MAGAHI FOLKORE AND FOLK TALES

MAGAHI FOLKLORE AND FOLK TALES

SHEELA VERMA

MANOHAR
2008

First published 2008

ISBN 978-81-7304-804-3

Published by
Ajay Kumar Jain *for*
Manohar Publishers & Distributors
4753/23 Ansari Road, Daryaganj
New Delhi 110 002

Typeset by
Kohli Print
Delhi 110 051

Printed at
Salasar Imaging Systems
Delhi 110035

Contents

Prefatory Notes

This book originates from my intense love for the Magahi culture and language. I present different facets of Magahi society, both in the abstract and as the backdrop for stories from my own life and experience in a Magahi-speaking family. Because my own experiences are so integral to the book, and the account of the Magahi-speaking world that I provide, I will relate my background and childhood in detail in this preface.

I spent my childhood in Gaya in the state of Bihar with my maternal grandparents. I was sent to a missionary convent school run by nuns and started speaking Hindi and English well. My grandparents used Magahi in conversation with me, making me a fluent Magahi speaker. My college schooling was done in Patna, the capital of Bihar, which is also a Magahi-speaking area.

By growing up in Magahi surroundings, I developed a great love for the Magahi culture. The fairs and festivals, religious observances, the rich and melodious Magahi songs all fascinated me greatly. The weddings we attended evoked great excitement in me. Even now, I remember these occasions very vividly.

I came to the United States in 1962 and have been here ever since. Of course, I visited India and Bihar very frequently, allowing me to collect data continually for this folklore book. My first book, *The Structure of the Magahi Verb* (1985), which emanated from my Ph.D. dissertation, also reflected my intense interest in the Magahi language.

My maternal grandfather (naanaa) was a deputy magistrate during the British Raj (Rule) and lived in Gaya with my maternal grandmother (naanii). He owned a lot of land and had built many houses in a large compound. His house was very large and comfortable with its own gate and wire fence. Naanaa was very unassuming and modest in his personality, but was quite brilliant in his profession. He took long walks, even in the intense heat of the summer season, although he owned a car of old model. He was a man of very simple habits. Even his food was also simple under my naanii's supervision.

Naanii was regal in her personality. She was very fair and tall with delicate features. My own mother resembled her strongly. Naanii never cooked herself but was surrounded by Magahi cooks and servants. Naanaa's breakfast, which was served at seven, consisted of fried puffed *puris* (unleavened bread fried in ghee), *bhujia* made of potatoes or any green vegetable (such as okra), and *halwa* (a sweet dish). His lunch was basmati rice, dal (lentil soup), two or three curries, and home made ghee and curds. His early dinner again served at six in the evening consisted of delicious *puris*, *bhujia*, curds and sweets. No one in India but my naanaa ate dinner that early. He woke up at five in the morning and would take a hot bath and do the *Geeta paath* (recitation from the holy book *Geeta*). He went to bed at eight or nine. He never went to parties and feasts. He was a total vegetarian, as was my naanii—neither of them even ate onions or garlic.

Naanaa was a theosophist, as were my parents. They would attend conventions held in Varanasi and Adyar, Madras. I remember their travels as fun. I used to travel with them in my childhood and enjoyed myself very much. The place where this convention took place in Varanasi was called the Theosophical Society. It had large beautiful gardens. I remember beautiful trees everywhere with large oranges hanging in them. My naanii used to carry a tall cooker with her to cook food. As she never cooked herself, the cook would travel with us. The tall cooker consisted of three or four compartments to make rice, dal, and curry simultaneously. The bottom part was a charcoal stove attached to the cooker. Despite this traveling convenience, the fun part was to visit the small stalls of food in the convention where one could buy delicacies to eat.

Naanaa and naanii lived lavishly in their home. The house was a real work of love, and naana's skill and care for the details went into it. It was in a big compound, and our front verandah overlooked a lawn surrounded by flowerbeds and evergreens. Here male visitors were received. On the other side was a verandah where meals were served except on winter evenings. The kitchen and the courtyard facing the verandah was the women's domain, with rooms and storerooms. There were servants' quarters, spacious kitchen gardens, and a small orchard. Naanaa was not generous in spending money, and the furnishings of his house were pretty simple. He had a Kashmiri rug, which must have come from his travels in Kashmir, in his living room with a couple of sofas and chairs. The pictures in the room consisted of naanaa's small family and paintings.

On the other side in the compound there were small houses, not bungalows, but comfortable homes nonetheless, all patterned alike. They had kitchens, bedrooms, courtyards, and verandahs facing the courtyards. These houses were rented. There were builders working in these homes all the time, fixing and changing the homes under naanaa's supervision. People called naanaa 'Deputy Sahib'. He did not seem to trust his workers and therefore he was supervising the builders all the time. He would be with the workers for hours during near freezing winter days as well as in summer heat, although the enormous thick compound walls were there to protect against heat.

In the dry climate the upkeep of such a well-built house was quite easy. Of course, the garden required constant and continuous attention. I am not talking of big orchards which naanaa had by the side of his houses. For these, he had farmer guards. These orchards included every variety of fruit that could grow in Bihar. The vegetable garden was near the kitchen, and naanii, with the help of servants, looked after it. All manner of seasonal vegetables, such as cauliflower, okra, squash, and cabbage, grew in the garden. Naanii took pride in providing them for the family lunches and dinners.

Naanaa began his day early. He would go for long walks even in hot weather. He had a lot of land in a nearby village called Karamkilla near Gaya. He would go for long walks in this village to see his crops. He used to visit this place with my naanii. Naanii would go wearing man's clothes, *kurta*, *pyjamas* with a turban, for in that village, women never went to the fields. Naanaa also taught her a script that only he could read, no one else. When naanaa wrote her letters only she could read them.

Naanaa had two daughters who were married to two brothers of the same family. The older brother was sent to England by my naanaa to study and he came back as a barrister. My father, the younger brother, was never sent to England though he very much wanted to go. Unfortunately, my aunt—my mother's older sister—and my uncle—my father's older brother—died in small pox epidemic just after my uncle had just returned from England and had started practice as a barrister. After their death, my naanaa and naanii raised their two sons. My mother remained naanaa's only child. I had two older sisters and an older brother. Naanaa had a very good time playing with his grandchildren. He used to read us the *Illustrated Weekly of India*, a very prestigious magazine, and ordered many scientific things by mail. He got a great kick out of these things.

He once ordered a toy gun that fascinated him a great deal, and my brother accidentally shot near naanaa's ear. The sound was so loud that he almost became hard of hearing but he never regretted it. Naanaa was a very quiet person by nature. He did not have many friends. Most of the time he was in his large room reading, and sometimes talking to himself. He communicated with his grandchildren very well, but he did not always communicate much with naanii.

During my stay, Naanii indulged me a lot. I had a passion for clothes in my childhood which I must have inherited from my mother, and which I have to this day. Once, I wanted an orange satin dress, and naanii went to a shop in downtown Gaya, bought the fabric, called her *darzi* (tailor), and got it stitched. I was overjoyed. Naanii's tailor also used to make my uniform. I wore my uniform—white blouse and navy blue skirt and 'Bata' shoes and white socks—to my convent school. Naanii also had a favorite jeweler who used to visit her from time to time. I used to get gold bangles, earrings, and other trinkets as Dussehra and Holi gifts. Naanii used to make cloth dolls (*guriaa*) beautifully. I had a good collection of them.

I also remember taking these dolls to a mango orchard on very hot afternoons. The afternoons in the months of April and May were very hot, because the gust of *loo* (hot wind) used to blow with enough strength to make anyone sick. I would manage to sneak out in the orchard. My friends would join me. Naanaa had large mango and fruit orchards. They looked pretty when large mangoes or guavas or bananas or apples would hang from the trees. Guards watched over these fruits carefully. At this time our schools, as well as offices and shops, were closed at noontime. We had morning sessions. We used to sneak out to the mango orchards and play with our cloth dolls and had a lot of fun until we got interrupted. The watchman would go and complain to my mother. We would be punished.

Naanii had a beautiful vegetable and herb garden that she took pride in supervising. Naanaa's meals consisted of those vegetables most of the time—her specialty was the crisp *ramturai* (okra) *bhujia* (deep fried in ghee) with round puffed puris was quite a treat for all of us. Gardening was naanii's continuous interest, but she also used to recite the *Ramayana* and sing sonorous Magahi devotional songs everyday.

Another remarkable thing about naanii was her excessive kind-heartedness. No one could stay hungry in her house, be they family member or an outsider. Her philosophy was that food must be offered to them at any cost. She always offered them her delicacies. Every summer during the *loo* days she would get a tent built by the side of a wide charred street under a dense *peepal* tree in front of our compound. In the tent there were many gigantic pitchers of cold water and soaked *kaalaa chana* (black gram) in huge containers to feed the passersby. Sometimes they had roasted gram flour, which was called *sattu*, with raw mango pieces. They used to make *sattu* dough on a leaf plate and eat it with zest. I liked to spend time in the tent. The huge *peepal* tree with its branches spread around was the coolest place in the compound, as it provided a soft and cool breeze to the tent. Maybe my naanii did all this to be able to earn good merits by feeding the poor and the fastest way to reach heaven.

Once a week—generally on Sundays when everyone was home—her *naun* (barber's wife) would come and do manicure and also pedicure with her tools. The women and girls would surround the *naun*, who would apply *mahavar* or *altaa* on the upper portion of the feet of all the women on all religious and festive occasions. *Altaa* is the soft and pleasing red colored liquid that is drawn into designs such as creepers, flowers, and *swastika*. *Altaa* is used by 'blessedly married' (*suhagin*) women on auspicious occasions.

Naanii had *mehendi* (*henna*) plants in her garden. The *naun* would bring freshly ground *mehendi* and apply it to the hands of the ladies and girls. It was quite a ritual. The *naun* would sing devotional or seasonal songs in Magahi and everyone joined her. By the early evening the *naun* and the *naaii* (barber) would take leave with money and lots of food and clothes. The *naaii* came to give men a haircut, pedicure and manicure, but women did not cut their hair.

My naanaa believed in the education of women, despite the prevailing norms against it at the time. My mother was schooled privately due to the lack of educational facilities for women. In line with his beliefs, she passed matriculation (high school) and later she obtained an Intermediate degree as well as a B.A. My father also helped her get the degrees. My mother had a great influence on me. In Gaya she became the headmistress (principal) of Girls High School and helped girls pass matriculation examinations.

My naanaa helped her run this school. He supported many of the school's expenses. Quite a few cousins of mine graduated from this school along with hundreds of girls of that area.

My mother was regarded highly because she was not only highly educated in relation to my father's large joint family, but also to the entire Bihari community. She was the first female graduate in the state of Bihar. She learned the art of managing a high school in Gaya. Later, she moved to Patna where my father lived. I also came to Patna for my further education.

My mother continued to do social and political jobs. She became the president of All India Women's Conference of Bihar branch, a position that she held for many years. She opened two schools, one high school and the other for destitute women. A lot of women from villages came and joined in. These were mostly Magahi women. They learned, exhibited, and sold all kinds of folk arts, including various kinds of bamboo work, terracotta, Magahi painting, cloth crafts, appliqué crafts, and hand embroidery.

My mother was impressive looking. She wore silk *saris* and shoes with heels that were available in Westernized shops. As she was a theosophist, she would visit conventions and All India Women's Conferences and buy beautiful *saris*. Some of them were heavy silk with beautiful colors of contrast borders. Some were imported also. She gave up using imported *saris* and shoes after the Satyagrah movement by Mahatma Gandhi. She started wearing *khadi* (hand-woven) *saris* and blouses and simple flat chappals. She became active politically and socially and became a MLC, or a member of Legislature. She continued to be active for quite some time.

Much later, when naanaa and naanii grew very old, they moved to Patna. My mother rented an apartment for them close to our house. My mother took care of them with the help of servants. Naanii passed away first, and then naanaa also died. He kept his desire to be able to live for a hundred years to see the scientific progress of the world.

On the other side of my family, my paternal grandfather (we called him baabaa) was a big zamindar with an overpowering personality who lived in a village called Dona in Gaya district. My daadii (paternal grandmother) died before I was born—I did not get to see her. Baabaa built a mansion in Dona. He used to sit in the living room of his huge house. He lived in the outer section of his house. He had a large *kalamdan* (a large metal box for pens) in front of him. It contained pens and ink in different sections of the box. It also contained lots of money in other sections. When we children went to see him he would give us a few *annas* (16 *annas* made a rupee) and we would be overjoyed.

Dona house was a beautiful, huge concrete house. It was a mansion standing in the middle of that village. The house was impressive, especially in comparison to the neighboring houses of our relatives, which were not that beautiful. It had large rooms and a large kitchen. The outer section was built for men as a living hall.

We would take the train to the house. From the railway station, we would travel by elephants or palanquins to the house, because there were no paved roads for buses and cars. Now, of course, paved road has been built to get to the village; I am talking of the days before *zamindari* was abolished. My grandfather had a lot of property and two or three elephants would sit at the entrance and guard the house. The house was well decorated. I still remember the hand-pulled ceiling fans made of colorful satin in every room. These were fans decorated with colorful satin with gold embroidery. They were hooked on the ceiling of the large rooms with heavy ropes. A person outside the rooms would sit and pull it. It generated soothing air and atmosphere for the people who slept in the room.

The month of *Savan* (July–August) was a gay month of rains. Before the rains, nights became hot and still, and summer gathered full strength. Dust storms would arrive, followed by cooling shower. The parched soil cracked. The air too was so dry that one could easily drink a large pitcher of water. At this time the rain would fall with its soothing effect with fragrant smell of moist dust. The sky became covered with white and dark clouds. The large drops of rain will start dropping. The frogs croaked, relieved by the heat. The farmers rejoiced with this summer rain. The wet smell would last for three or four days and then sun would shine bright in the blue sky. It was the month for picnics, songs and celebrations.

The autumn became chillier but the leaves didn't fall. The sun would rise like a big orange in a clear sky. Days were crystal clear. There was much work in the fields and neighboring villages. Many crops grew in these winter months. Sugar cane came in November but wheat, barley, grams, peas, and mustard came in winter. Winter was also very pleasant in Dona. We used warm hand made *sujinis* (beautiful silk quilts) to cover ourselves. Near the town there was a big market for the crops that grew in the village. While men (farmers) at this time worked in the fields, the women grew busy spinning and stitching and sang together.

Bihar has five seasons: winter, spring, summer, rains and autumn. I am reminded of a few common sights in my village. One of the sights was women walking from the wells with pitchers on their heads filled with water. They walked along narrow banks, talking and laughing with their bodies swaying rhythmically without dropping even a drop of water from the pitchers on their heads. Another typical sight that was very interesting was women walking at noon to fields carrying food or goods on their heads. They carried flat cane baskets on their heads with thick baked *tava* (iron skillet) *roti* of wheat or corn with some cooked vegetables for their farmer husbands. This was also the season of healthy appetite for rich food. Dona's food was rich with ghee, curds and buttermilk, and of course green vegetables that grew in the fields. We consumed unleavened bread called *parathas* made in a *tava* with a lot of pure ghee.

Farmers' wives cooked vegetables everyday, some time deep-fried in ghee and sometimes cooked with freshly ground *masala* paste. They used a large *sil* and *lorhha* (flat stone grinder) in which they ground their fresh *masala* everyday. The dry ground *masalas*, which are available nowadays, were unheard of then. Then, the *masalas* were mostly home grown turmeric, coriander seeds, garlic, onions and mustard seeds. Turmeric paste was very special for split pea dal and vegetables. Special sweets, *kheer* (rice pudding) and carrot *halwa* were made in this season. Most of these could last through extreme weather conditions. These included *shakarpala*, *rewdi*, *laddu* of besan and wheat flour made with sugar or jaggery. Sweets made of milk—*barfi*, *gulabjamun* and *pera*—were available in the *halwai*, or confectioners' shops. They were very popular. Farmers' wives used to be busy making *vadian* (lentil balls) and different kinds of pickles of mangoes sweet and sour. These were preserved for us to eat on festive occasions when we assembled in Dona for vacation, festivals or weddings.

When baabaa grew old, he moved to Gaya with his older son, and passed away a few years later. baabaa had four sons, including my father, and one daughter. The joint family members (male and female) who lived with baabaa also helped raise the children. My father decided to move to the city of Patna during the lifetime of my baabaa.

My father was a self-made man. He was an attorney (advocate) in Patna High Court and also a professor of law in Patna Law College. He belonged to a very large joint family, but did not believe in living within a joint family. He did not want to live in Dona or Gaya. He moved to Patna at a very young age, where he rented a house and started studying and meeting the expenses of running a house in the city and educating his cousins. He helped them move to Patna for high school and college education. All the younger generation at that time came to Patna. My family got educated with two district judges, lawyers, and professors filling its ranks. My father was tall, fair and very erect in his personality. He was strong, bold, outspoken, fearless and tough. He spoke English very well, was quite an orator. He loved to give speeches and talks in conferences and conventions. He also wrote very well. He never failed to write for magazines and newspapers. My mother was more engrossed in politics than he was. He was tied in his profession and trying to build-up a lucrative practice. Most of his practice came from neighboring villages or Muslim clients. He was a staunch Theosophist, a true follower of Annie Besant and Krishnamurti who believed in the knowledge of divine things, god, wisdom and Divine Being obtained by spiritual ecstasy. He was not a traditional worshipper of all gods. He was religious, a follower of one god, but he did not like rituals which priests preached. He would read the *Geeta*, and the book *At the Feet of the Master* published by the Theosophical Publishing House. In his later years he read the *Ramayana* on my mother's insistence. He was also greatly influenced by Dr. Aurandale who had come to India from England and taught theosophy ideals very well and coherently. Dr. Aurandale had stayed in India for quite some time and had married Rukminiji, the famous Bharatnatyam dancer.

My mother also believed in the teachings of theosophy but also observed all the Hindu religious festivals and deities. She also believed in the preaching of a family *panditji* (Hindu priest). My mother was very impressed with Rukminiji. She came to Patna to perform a Bharatnatyam dance. My parents organized it. She wore beautiful south Indian Kalakshetra *saris* of heavy silk and wide borders. She looked stunningly beautiful. I remember my mother when she went to Adyar in south India to attend Theosophical conventions bought quite a few saris of that kind. At that time those saris were considered very new in style and fashion.

My father had very simple taste in his clothes. He continually advocated simplicity in clothes, food and thought. After the Satyagrah movement of Gandhiji it became still more simpler. He also switched to *khadi kurta*, *dhoti* and woolen *shervani* in winter. I think he also had a Gandhi cap when he went for walks. But when he went to argue his cases in Patna High Court he wore black blazer, white cotton shirt and pants and white bow in place of a necktie. He was very health conscious and was very particular about nutritional food. My father used to visit naanaa's house frequently because my mother's older sister was married to my father's older brother. That led to my father's marriage with my mother. He later became quite an intellectual and spent mutual time-sharing with my mother. They wanted to see the west. In fact, my father wanted to go to England for his higher studies like his older brother, but he could not go.

My parents never saw America. I was working hard at that time and my parents were getting older. They would have loved to visit USA and would have appreciated its advancement and progress. My intense desire was to bring them here and show them the country in which I resided, but it never came true. I am glad my first book, *The Structure of the Magahi Verb* (1985), was dedicated to them. They were very pleased with it. My mother died at the age of 89 and father died when he was 91.

I came to the United States in 1962. I enrolled in a graduate program in English at the University of Michigan, Ann Arbor and received my Master degree in 1965. Subsequently I started teaching Hindi in the Department of South Asian Studies at the University of Wisconsin, Madison. Currently this department is known as Department of Languages and Cultures of Asia. In addition to teaching courses in Hindi I became very interested in researching aspects of the Magahi language. The topic of my Ph.D. dissertation was the structure of the Magahi verb. I also became interested in the folklore aspects of Magahi. During that period, a series of talks on folklore were organized at the University of Wisconsin in Madison. The late professor A.K. Ramanujan was one of the speakers in the series and all the lectures that I attended inspired me to take up the study of Magahi folklore intensely. Some of his books on folklore, such as *Folktales from India* (New York, 1991), *A Flowering Tree* (California Press, 1997), gave me a lot of insight into this subject matter. I also got a chance to attend courses on folklore by Professor Niels Ingwerson. Those lectures gave me ideas as to how to structure my projected work on Magahi folklore. Other colleagues—particularly V. Narayan Rao and A.K. Narain—encouraged me to undertake a book project on Magahi folklore.

Professor Manindra Verma, my husband, facilitated the

project in many ways, as did my daughter, Professor Mona Verma Makhija. Mona read my drafts and offered editorial suggestions enthusiastically despite her own professional commitments. I would also like to express my deep appreciation for the help that Sungok Hong provided in this project. Sungok, then a student in the Department of Languages and Cultures of Asia at the University of Wisconsin-Madison (and now a Lecturer in the India Studies Program at Indiana University-Bloomington) offered to type the manuscript despite her preoccupation with her teaching responsibilities and dissertation commitments at that time. Subsequently, Anjali Kaushlesh Dayal has provided useful editorial comments in finalizing the manuscript. She has had a wide range of experience as a senior staff reporter and copy/associate managing editor at the Columbia *Daily Spectator* when she was in college, and has subsequently been editing and teaching technical writing at the New York City Department of Education's program for aspiring principals. My deepest thanks and gratitude to them all.

SHEELA VERMA

PART I

MAGAHI FOLKLORE

Introduction

Magadh, as is well known, occupies a special place in the history of folklore. Folk dialects have preserved Magadh culture in folk songs, and tales, and other aspects of folklore. Folklore is embedded in jokes, proverbs, rhymes, tales, and other folk forms. In order to study the folklore one should not study only the written literature but also its oral tradition, since this is an important part of folklore. Folk literature comprises stories, ballads, and tales, among other forms, and is essentially an oral literature that travels all over the world, generation after generation, by word of mouth. T. Benfey's 1859 German translation of *Panchtantra* pointed out striking similarities between Sanskrit and European tale, allowing us to glimpse how tales undergo changes as they diffuse and migrate. The folk stories prevailing in Magadh are very close to the stories of *Panchtantra* and *Hitopadesha*. They have a wit and humor and beauty which is universal to folk stories, and which knows no state or national boundaries.

Religion and history have of course been vital underpinnings of the narrative art of storytelling. Most of the *vratas* are based on gods' and goddesses' stories. There are places in Bihar where the sage Valmiki resided and are associated with the stories of Rama and Sita. These stories are parts of Magadh more current in Rajgir, Nalanda and in Gaya. The role Magadh played in preserving early Indian folklore and tales is great. It was at Pataliputra (Patna) that Vishnu Sharma (fifth century) wrote fables, which found their way into Persian, Arabic, and Hebrew, Greek and Syrian languages. Magadh was one of the greatest dynasties that ever reigned in India in the past. The Mauryas, the Shungas and the Guptas were the kings who ruled Magadh over a great part of India. The capital of Magadh, Pataliputra remained the seat of learning for centuries.

India is alive with folklore. She is a country of yarns and legends, ghosts and superstition. Magadh is also in its footsteps. Her people have more folklore in their heads than a hundred books could hold. It is full of myths, fables and legends of various kinds. *Panchtantra* (fifth century) is the oldest book on fables. Before the origin of the *Panchtantra* the folk tales appear in Vedic literature. The Jatakas, which contain the stories of various incarnations of Lord Buddha, are full of instructive stories. The various beasts and birds play important part and teach a moral. The *Hitopadesha* is the popular book of Sanskrit fables composed by Narayan Pandit in the fourteenth century AD. Many of the stories in this book have been adapted from *Panchtantra*.

I was born in Gaya in the state of Bihar and was educated in Patna, the capital of Bihar. Bodh Gaya is famous because Lord Buddha attained enlightenment here and is a very important Hindu and Buddhist pilgrimage. I was raised in a Magahi-speaking area, and learned to speak fluently. Various other languages of the Magadhi Prakrit family of Bihar surround the Magahi-speaking area. In the north across the Ganges is Maithili, and across its western and southern borders is Bhojpuri. Magahi thus covers districts of Patna, Gaya, Hazaribagh, Munger, and Bhagalpur in the state of Bihar, and is the dominant language of South Bihar. As the name suggests, Magahi is related to Magadhi. Magahi originated from middle Indic Magadhi Prakrit, as have other languages of Bihar, Bengal, Assam and Orissa. I address this evolution in the 'Magahi Language' chapter of this book.

I grew up listening to Magahi folk tales, and to songs sung by my grandmother (naanii), and tried to save some of them. Modern grandmothers have not retained the folk traditions, and folk tales and other cultural folk items will be lost soon. Fortunately, we still have village grandmas who have retained stories and songs to safeguard our folk traditions. Aside from these grandmothers, not much is done to retain the rich oral tradition, and so these folk traditions, customs, observance songs (*vratas*), and tales need to be preserved before they disappear totally. The pressure facing the common man and the daily drudgery of living has affected the villagers also. Political turmoil has also influenced them, and they have started talking about politics instead of folkloric topics.

This book on Magahi folklore is the result of the great love I have developed for the culture from these stories, and in the course of my study of the language. This book is my attempt to address the decline of Magahi culture, as well as the dearth of studies on traditional Magadh culture and folklore. The disappearance of Magahi folklore or tales will be a definite loss to the Magahi society, and thereby a loss of Magahi history, customs, traditions and culture. I believe a serious attempt must be made now to collect and preserve the folklore items so that they are not totally lost. While studies on the Indian caste system, social structure, kinship, and village organization received the attention of both Western and Indian scholars; the study of oral tradition unfortunately has been neglected. In my opinion, scholars have failed to understand that the study of oral traditions could help retain the rich Magadh culture.

Magahi folk literature is very extensive and interesting, and some academic work has been done on it in the past. George Grierson, a renowned linguist, closely studied Bihar, Uttar Pradesh and Bengal. His contribution to the study of folklore is very important. In all probability, he was the first Englishman who recognized the value of folk songs and ballads. He published them in the *Journal of the Royal Asiatic Society of England* and in *Indian Antiquary* of India. He also edited some Bhojpuri and Magahi folk songs with notes and English translation in the *Journal of the Royal Asiatic Society of England* (vol. XVI, 1884). His voluminous work *The Linguistic Survey of India* (1903–7) contained a lot of oral narratives. Besides these he also wrote a very important book, *Bihar Peasant Life*, in which he collected a lot of tales and songs regarding Magahi and Bihar folklore. William Crooke, an English civilian in India, did a very systematic and informative book. The book is introduction to popular religion and folklore of northern India

(1894). This has been a major contribution to the study of folklore of Bihar and Magadh, and I draw on it in different chapters of this book.

I have been collecting and doing fieldwork for the past twenty years. My previous book *The Structure of the Magahi Verb* (1985) was also the result of this exploration. After that a lot of publications in Magahi came out. The most recent one was a chapter in *The Indo-Aryan Languages* edited by George Cardona and Dhanesh Jain (2003).

The basic structure and material of the book are as follows. The chapters on Magahi language give us the knowledge of the region and place where it is spoken. The chapter on Magahi Region and People provides the rich history of Magadh in some detail. The Magahi Weddings are also examined, alongside their rituals and songs, particularly the songs of abuse (*gaalii*). Rituals also form part of the chapters on Magahi folk songs and folk art (I discuss, for example, the way the birth of a child in a Magahi family is greeted with a particular tune of *sohar* songs). The chapter on the evil eye draws on Alan Dundes's book *The Evil Eye*, in which Dundes tells us of a superstition which is observed all over the world not only in India. The chapter on Birth, Death and Reincarnation are particularly interesting because they describe very different ceremonies than the usual ones in different cultures.

The chapters on Magahi ballads, folk tales, proverbs and riddles provide information on some important ballads. The stories were familiar to me from my early age. We used to gather with my joint family members in weddings in our village Dona near the city of Gaya and indulged in storytelling, riddling and many similar episodes. The section II in my book has Magahi folk tales. I have been collecting and listening to these stories. Some I read in Magahi folk tale books also. Ram Prasad Singh's collections in *Magadh ki Lok Kathaeñ* (1997) provided me a lot of insight. Sampatti Aryani has also given a very beautiful description of Magahi folklore in her book *Magahi Bhaashaa aur Saahitya* (1976).

Many chapters also include an ethnographic component

drawn from my own life. In this sense, this book is as much about the day-to-day living understandings of Magahi culture, as it is about folklore and tradition in the academic sense. I have enjoyed working on this book very much. I hope this provides inspiration to the readers of India as well as the readers of the West and they add more towards Magahi research. I hope the reconstruction of the past history of Magadh becomes the concern of people in the East and West.

Magahi Language

Introduction

Magahi is one of the three commonly recognized principal languages under the rubric of Bihari languages. Bhojpuri and Maithili are the other two. From the time of Grierson's survey (Grierson 1903–28), these languages have been assumed to represent one branch of an Eastern group of languages, namely, the Magadhi group of the Middle Indo-Aryan, which includes Bengali, Assamese, and Oriya. This view has generally been subscribed to by many scholars including Chatterji (1926) and Katre (1968). More recently, though, other scholars, such as Cardona (1974) and Jeffers (1976), have argued for a modified sub-grouping. Cardona attaches it to the Central group with Eastern Hindi and Western Hindi. Jeffers goes a step further and would prefer to posit a Bihari sub-group itself within New Indo-Aryan, independent of the Hindi languages on the one hand, and the Bengali languages on the other.

At any rate, the speakers of Magahi, and other Bihari languages, have a sense of identity, as well as a great deal of cultural affinity with the Hindi group in various ways. They very often will identify their language as Hindi in response to census questions, thereby skewing figures for the speakers of the language. Hindi is the formal language of the region, used in schools and law courts. Magahi today employs the Devanagari script borrowed directly from Hindi in place of the Kaithi script used earlier. Both in vocabulary and phonology, it has a greater alignment with eastern Hindi, as well as an inevitable lexical borrowing from the formal, administrative, and literary varieties of western Hindi as the state language. In morphology it has some crucial affinity with Bengali and the eastern group, though it has eastern flavors in some aspects of phonology, too. Within the Bihari group itself, from all accounts, Magahi and Maithili are closer together forming an eastern branch of the Bihari as opposed to Bhojpuri as its western branch.

Magahi Speech Area

Unlike Bhojpuri, which is prominently spoken in a significant portion of two Indian states—Bihar and Uttar Pradesh—Magahi is essentially restricted to the state of Bihar, now divided into Bihar and Jharkhand, though there are mixed varieties of the language found in the adjoining regions of Bengal and Orissa, too. The name Magahi is a direct derivative of the name Magadhi itself and many educated speakers of Magahi prefer to call it Magadhi rather than Magahi. Magahi, in the sense of the language of the Magadh country, covers the currently reorganized districts of Patna, Gaya, Nalanda, and Nawada in Bihar, which would roughly correspond to that historical territory, and so it does. This area may be interpreted as defining the focal area for what may be termed 'standard Magahi'. The description of the Magahi language relates to this standard variety of Magahi.

The total geographical area covered by Magahi today is, of course much larger. In a very broad sense, the river Ganga may be seen as marking a linguistic boundary making Magahi the language of South Bihar as opposed to Maithili as the language of north Bihar (with the river Son marking a western border to separate it from Bhojpuri). On the west it extends to the eastern part of the district of Palamu, on the east to portions of the districts of Munger and Bhagalpur, on the south to Singhbhum, and on the south-east to Dhanbad, all in the state of Bihar. Magahi does, however, extend beyond Bihar (even though marginally) into Bengal in the district of Purulia (which was part of the state of Bihar until 1956), and into Orissa in the districts of Mayurbhanj and Bamra. In fact, there is another region in Bengal, Malda in its northern part, where Magahi co-exists with Bengali. It is referred to in almost all discussions on Magahi, including Grierson (1903). Since this area is not contiguous to any other Magahi-speaking area, it is perhaps a case of migrant Magahi community, though there are other theories (Grierson 1903: 179; Pandeya 1980: 108).

Dialects of Magahi

Grierson (1903) and Aryani (1976) both identify two basic dialects of Magahi, standard Magahi and Eastern Magahi. From the focal area, standard Magahi, with possible local variations, extends to Aurangabad and the eastern border of Palamu on the west, and Hazaribagh and Giridih on the south and south-east. On the north-east, it extends to the western portions of the districts of Munger and Bhagalpur.

Eastern Magahi is the name given to a collection of sub-dialects on the eastern and southern border of south Bihar where Magahi meets Bengali (in Purulia) and Oriya (in Mayurbhanj and Bamra). It starts along the eastern border of the Ranchi plateau and goes through the Bengali-speaking Manbhum area and then turns west, skirting the southern part of the plateau through the Oriya elements of Singhbhum. The Magahi of Malda in upper Bengal is also treated by Grierson (1905) as part of Eastern Magahi. In addition, Eastern Magahi is also spoken in the south-east of Hazaribagh, in the extreme east of the Ranchi district, and in Kharsawan of the Singhbhum district, and all of them have been heavily influenced by their neighboring languages. While the regional varieties of Standard Magahi are all called Magahi, the sub-dialects of Eastern Magahi have various names. The prominent ones are KuRmali in Mayurbhanj and Kharsawan, KuRmali Thar, KhoTTa in the Manbhum region, Sadri Kol in Bamra, KhonTai in Malda, and Paanch Parganiaa or Tamariaa in the extreme east of the Ranchi district. Each name has its own logic, which also allows for the name 'Hindi' (as opposed to Bengali) in Malda, and 'Bengal' (because of heavy borrowing and the script from Bengali) in the south-east of the Hazaribagh district, in addition to the usual name Magahi or Magahiyaa as in the Dhanbad area.

Speakers of Magahi

It is not easily possible to indicate the number of Magahi speakers for the simple reason that dependable statistics are not available. This is so because of two reasons: in the standard Magahi region, in response to census questions, most educated speakers of Magahi name Hindi as their language since that is what they use in formal contexts and so consider it to be the appropriate response. Additionally, the uneducated and the rural population of Magahi speakers return Hindi, as the generic name for their language. In the Eastern Magahi area, as discussed above, sub-dialectal names as KuRmaali, KhoTTa, Paanch Parganiaa and even Hindi used more often than Magahi in census responses.

Aryani (1965), on the basis of several data, estimated the number of Magahi speakers at approximately 9,900,000 for 1951. Surprisingly enough, the 1971 census figures show only 6,638,495 speakers for Magahi. This discrepancy can be understood in the context of the socio-linguistic phenomenon of educated urban speakers naming their language of schooling, Hindi, as their mother-tongue. Obviously, the number of Magahi speakers did not really decline between 1951 and 1971 but was simply swallowed up by the census figures for Hindi. Breton (1997) estimates the number at 9 million. Grimes (1996), however, provides the figure 10,821,000 for 1994, and further gives Magahi the 75th position among the top 100 languages of the world by population, with the figure of 12 million speakers as currently updated.

Scripts and Literary Tradition

In one sense, Magahi is written in four scripts: Devanagari, Kaithi, and also Bengali and Oriya. The Bengali and Oriya scripts are, of course, employed in writing the forms of Eastern Magahi current in the Manbhum area, such as Purulia but also in the south-eastern part of the Hazaribagh district that borders on the Manbhum region. The Oriya script is used, expectedly, in areas where it co-exists with Oriya, such as Mayurbhanj. Devanagari is, of course, the script for personal communication, and sometimes in semi-legal transactions. The Kaithi script gets its name from the word 'Kayath' < 'Kayastha', the caste of writers in northern India, and has been current until recently in Bihar and eastern Uttar Pradesh. It derives from early Nagari and is closely related to the current Gujarati script, which replaced the Devanagari only in the nineteenth century.

In terms of written production, there has been some effort on the part of the scholars in the Magahi area to explore and identify a literary tradition for Magahi and, in fact, to go as far back as the Siddha Sahitya of the eight century, and the subsequent Nathpanth Sahitya and the Sand Sahitya traditions the same way as Hindi literature does (e.g. Aryani 1976: 28–31, Pandeya 1982, Singh 1982). More relevantly, Magahi is quite rich in its folk literature, and in modern times, there have been various activities in the publication of creative writing. A great deal of enthusiasm has been shown in organizing literary activities. An organization called Magahi Parishad was established in Patna in 1952, and was later renamed Bihar Magahi Mandal. A monthly journal called *Magadhi* was started at the same time, and was later renamed *Bihaan*. Both these events have been in the nature of growing efforts towards the linguistic and literary promotion of Magahi.

A Phonological Sketch of Magahi

The phonological sketch of Magahi is very close to the phonological system of Hindi. In fact, it is because of this reason, among some other important ones, that laymen perceive Magahi as an offshoot of Hindi, even though it is genetically closer to Bengali. When we refer to the phonology of Hindi being very close to Magahi, we are referring to the historically developed form of Hindi. The historically developed forms (*tadbhava*) in Hindi have lost the three way sibilant distinction /sh/, /S/, and /s/ and have retained only /s/. The forms with /sh/ that we find in Hindi today are all loan words from Sanskrit or Persian. Similarly, the five-way distinction in the nasals has been reduced to two /m/ and /n/. This is not to say that / /, / / and the retroflex /N/ do not occur. They do but only allophonically before homorganic velar, palatal and retroflex sounds respectively. Magahi does exactly the same thing. However, unlike Hindi (or Urdu), Magahi has not borrowed any sounds from Sanskrit and Persian, though it has borrowed words. This borrowing of sounds has reinstituted sounds like /sh/, /S/, / / and / /in Hindi and introduced new ones like /k, kh, g, z, f/. The words of Sanskrit and Persian borrowed in Magahi are phonologically reshaped to conform to the phonology of Magahi.

Thus,	Sanskrit	doSa;	Hindi	dosh	Magahi	dos
	Persian	s'ahr	Hindi	shahar	Magahi	sahar
	Persian	roz	Hindi	roz	Magahi	roj
	Sanskrit	guNa	Hindi	guN	Magahi	gun, etc.

Magahi Region and People

As previously noted, Magahi is associated with the ancient land of Magadh in the present state of Bihar to the south of the river Ganges. Magadh occupies a very important place in the history of this area, and indeed in the history of all of India. The Aryans took several centuries to spread eastwards along the Ganga Valley. They reached northern Bihar around 700 BC (Jogesh Das 1973). There is literary evidence of this in the *Ramayana* and the *Mahabharata*, which are estimated to date from 500 BC and 400 AD (Stanley Wolpert 1989). References in ancient literatures like the Vedas and the Puranas, other epics and a host of archaeological discoveries tell us that the history of Magadh dates back a couple of thousand years.

First, some background on the relevant sources: one earliest literary source is the *Rig Veda*, dating from roughly 1200 BC. The remaining Vedic literature—the *Sama*, *Yajur* and *Atharva Vedas*—are from later dates. A historical reconstruction of Aryan life and institutions is based on this literature. The epics the *Ramayana* and the *Mahabharata* are concerned with events that took place between 1000 BC and 700 BC (Romila Thapar 1968). The *Mahabharata* is the longest single poem in the world, and was crafted by Vyas, a Brahmin poet. It is episodic in nature, and mentions Magadh and the Magadh people. The main action revolves around the famous struggle at Kurukshetra between the Kauravas and the Pandavas over land rights. Among the other episodes recounted within the text, the reign of the powerful King Jarasandh's reign receives elaborate attention. Jarasandh made Rajgir, which is in Magadh, his capital. In Rajgir, he built a Shiva temple and there locked a lot of kings in order to kill them and offer them to God as a sacrifice. Jarasandh earned the title of 'King of

Demons' from this action, and his family reigned in Magadh for nearly a thousand years.

Magadh is directly mentioned in the *Ramayana* also. The *Ramayana* is shorter than the *Mahabharata* and has fewer episodes. The original composer was the famous poet Valmiki. Rama, the son and heir of Dashratha, the king of Kosala, married Sita, the princess of Videha. Rama's stepmother Kaikeyi wanted her own son Bharata to be the king and succeeded in sending Rama, Sita and his younger brother Lakshmana into exile for fourteen years; the *Ramayana* is the story of this exile, its ordeals, and Rama's glorious return and reign. Magadh's powerful and organized administration is mentioned in Valmiki's *Ramayana*. The priest Vishwamitra was traveling to Videha with Rama and Lakshmana and Rama was very impressed when he saw a very organized and beautiful city of Videha, the seat of his future father-in-law, King Janak. South of Videha, on the right bank of the river Ganges, was the region of Magadh that was then still remote to many. It was not wholly Aryanized. People did not follow Vedic rites, and they roamed the land with their flocks and herds.

Later, in the time of Buddha under the great King Bimbisar (*c.* 540–490 BC), Magadh began to develop rapidly, and became a very powerful Indian empire. Magadh prospered and established itself as a center of political activity in northern India, a position it maintained for quite some time. Bimbisar was the earliest of the Indian kings to stress the need for efficient administration, and his son Ajatshatru anxiously sought to rule Magadh. He murdered his father in 490 BC and became king. He was determined to follow his father's policy of expansion through military conquest. During his reign, the capital of Magadh was at Rajgir, the very beautiful city that also held a key place in the *Mahabharata*.

Ajatshatru strengthened Rajgir, and built a fort in the vicinity of the Ganges. This later became Pataliputra. At this time, Magadh was recognized the most powerful kingdom in eastern India. Natural resources were also then in abundance in Magadh. The soil was rich and fertile for cultivation, and the neighboring forests gave timber for building and elephants for the army and offered many facilities (A.L. Basham 1954), which contributed to the region's strengthening under Ajatshatru.

Ajatshatru died in 461 BC. The people of Magadh appointed a viceroy, Shishunag, as king. Shishunag's dynasty did not last very long. Its successors, the Nandas, have been described as India's first empire builders. They inherited the large kingdom of Magadh and tried to expand it further. They established Magadh as a very important empire. But this was cut short by Chandragupta Maurya, the young, ambitious and dynamic king of Magadh and contemporary of Alexander the Great (324–301 BC). Both Indian and classical sources note that Chandragupta overthrew out the last of the Nandas and occupied their capital, Pataliputra. They also add that after Alexander's retreat Chandragupta subdued the north-west, driving out the Greeks. He spent the last quarter century of his life extending Magadh's power to Indus and beyond, and his reign was called the golden age.

Pataliputra was then a large city, surrounded beautifully by a wooden wall. It was established by Ajatshatru, and saw the rise and fall of India's major kingdom. The city became a famous Mauryan metropolis first under Chandragupta Maurya, and then under his grandson Ashoka. By writers of the time, Pataliputra is mentioned as the home of culture, learning and fine arts, and as the queen of the cities of the world. It was the home of learning and wealth. Its prestige was something unique, undoubtedly it dominated the intellectual life of India for many centuries. Megasthenes, the ambassador sent by Seleucus, stayed in Pataliputra for many years and wrote about the city in 302 BC. Megasthenes much admired the emperor Chandragupta for his keen insight in the administration of justice which he presided over personally in open *darbar* (court).

Other emperors who ruled from Pataliputra were Guptas and the Pala kings. Its period of glory spanned a thousand years from sixth century BC to fifth century AD. Today the city of Patna, the capital of Bihar state, is an important business center of eastern India. More significantly, it is a gateway to the Buddhist and Jaina pilgrim centers of Rajgir, Nalanda, Bodh Gaya, Pawapuri and Vaishali

Once a great city, Rajgir today is just a village, but vestiges of a legendary past remain. Located in a dense valley surrounded by rocky hills near Patna, Rajgir's historic importance to multiple religions is today what draws most of its visitors and its fame. It was in Rajgir that Lord Buddha spent many months of retreat devoted to meditation, and where he delivered some of his famous sermons and converted king Bimbisar of the Magadh kingdom.

Bodh Gaya, 13 kilometers from Gaya town, is the holiest among holy places where the quest of prince Siddharth reached enlightenment after years of seeking truth. He attained the supreme enlightenment and became the Buddha, or 'the enlightened one'. Bodh Gaya has naturally developed into the most sacred spot for Buddhism in all the world. It is situated on the bank of river Falgu. Gaya is a very important center of Hindu pilgrimage where people go to offer oblation for the salvation of their dead forefathers. It also attracts a lot of pilgrims who visit the famous temple of Vishnupad.

Other locations within Magadh also have world historical importance. Lord Mahavir spent 14 years of his life at Rajgir and at Nalanda. The Jainas, followers of Mahavir, claim that towards the end of his life Chandragupta was converted to Jainism and became an ascetic and fasted to death in the manner of Jaina saints. Chandragupta was succeeded by his son Bindusar (297 BC) and in 269 BC Bindusar was succeeded by his son Ashoka, the greatest ruler India has ever known. He also was one of the greatest kings of the world. Mauryan King Ashoka came in around 270 BC. After the Kalinga war Ashoka became a staunch Buddhist. Under his rule, Magadh became strong and powerful. He was the first of India's emperors to establish a set of firm tenets for the governance of people for his kingdom. He had these tenets inscribed on stone pillars which were put up across his kingdom. The pillars were crowned with the statue of one or more lions sitting on top of a pedestal which was inscribed with symbols of wheels. The lion denoted strength, the wheel denoted the eternal nature of truth (*dharma*), hence the name of *dharma chakra*.

This figure of lions, atop a pedestal, with inscription of a wheel was adopted as the official seal of the independent Republic of India in 1947. Ashoka's *dharma chakra* was incorporated into the national flag of India, the Indian tricolor. Ashoka was responsible also for widespread proselytization of people in Buddhism. He sent his son Mahendra and daughter Sanghmitra for this as far south as the present country of Sri Lanka. It was in Ashoka's reign that Buddhism ceased to be a simple Indian sect and began its evolution as a world religion. A great council of Buddhist clergy was held at Pataliputra, and after which missions were sent to various parts of India and beyond. For some fifty years Mauryan kings continued to rule Magadh until about 183 BC.

After the Mauryas, the Shunga Empire was established. Pushyamitra Shunga, a Brahmin general, succeeded in gaining power through a palace revolution. During his reign, the scholar Patanjali (the creator of *Yoga Sutra* and the science of yoga) perhaps came to Magadh and established himself there for some time. Magadh continued to be the center of scholarship for a long time.

After the Shunga dynasty fell, the Gupta dynasty ruled in Magadh. The Guptas were empire-builders, and controlled north India for over a hundred years. Chandragupta I became the king, and strove to restore the grandeur of the Mauryas. Magadh shone once again. Under Chandragupta's successor, Samudragupta (*c.* AD 335–76), Pataliputra once more became the center of a great empire. During the reign of Samudragupta's son Chandragupta II (*c.* AD 376–415), north India reached the heights of ancient Indian culture. Kalidas, the famous poet and dramatist, produced epics at this time. At this time, Pataliputra was also the region's seat of learning. The University of Nalanda was established there by Chandragupta's son Kumargupta I.

The university of Nalanda did not confine itself to training Buddhist monks but also taught other subjects. The monastery consisted of a very large complex of buildings, could accommodate large number of monks, and had facilities for 10,000 students, according to the Chinese traveler Hsuan Tsang. Other sources reveal courses of study included Buddhism scriptures (of both Hinayana and Mahayana schools), Vedas, *Hetu Vidya* (logic), *Shabda Vidya* (grammar), *Chikitsa Vidya* (medicine), etc. The University also received the royal patronage of Kannauj and Pala kings.

Today's Nalanda, where the ruins of the great university have been excavated, is situated at a distance of 90 kilometers south-east of Patna by road. The famous Chinese traveler Fahsien was in India for some six years in the beginning of the fifth century, during which he wrote a magnificent travelogue that describes some of his time in Magadh and at Nalanda.

Subsequently, the Pala dynasty began in Magadh. The reign of the great king Dharampal (*c.* AD 770–810) marks the height of Pala power. King Dharampal founded Vikramshila University, an enclave of scholars and disciples surrounded by large stone walls. The king generously endowed it with magnificent grants. The authorities and scholars who administered the university also looked after the Nalanda University, and both prospered at that time. The Pala kings were chiefly notable for their patronage of Buddhism, which flourished remarkably during the three centuries of their rule. Their capital became Uddantpur, which is now known as Biharsharif. Pataliputra, now Patna, was about 64 kilometers to the south of Uddantpur.

Govindpal, the last emperor, was defeated by Bakhtiyar Khilzi in AD 1191, and a Muslim reign started in Bihar and the Magadh region. They destroyed Nalanda and killed Buddhist monks. Centuries of Magadh's culture and scholarship were destroyed when invaders burned ancient libraries to the ground.

By the end of the twelfth century, Magadh leadership was in constant fluctuation. Gayasuddin Tughlaq was the first Muslim ruler in Bihar, and he changed the name of Darbhanga in Mithila to Tughlaqabad.

The Mughals came by 1526. Babur made Bihar a tributary with his victory at Panipat. Delhi's hold, however, was not strong during Mughal rule. Shershah was a powerful ruler of Bihar around 1545, and was eventually defeated by Akbar. Today, Shershah's tomb, Shershah Makbara, is in the town of Sasaram in Bihar.

British rule was established in Bihar around 1765. Thereafter, until the Sepoy Mutiny in 1857, Magadh was very disorganized. The social structure of the different parts of Bihar did not subsequently undergo much change during the political turmoil and the change of reigns that gripped the subcontinent. Today, the Magahi region is predominantly a part of the present state of Bihar, but technically during much of the British rule it was a part of the administrative unit of the Presidency of Bengal, which then encompassed the entirely to present-day Bihar itself, along with Bengal and Orissa. In 1912 the partition of Bengal created Bihar as a separate political unit. Later, under the Government of India Act of 1935, the Division of Orissa became a separate province, and the Division of Bihar came into being as a separate province and administrative unit of British India. This division separated some Magahi-speaking regions in Bihar and Orissa, notably in Mayurbhanj and Bamra.

At Independence in 1947, Bihar became a state of the Republic of India. Some south-east parts of Bihar, predominantly the district of Purulia, were separated and incorporated with West Bengal as part of the linguistic reorganization of Indian states. As a result of this in fact some linguistic areas of Magahi have now become part of the modern state of Bengal, alongside the Magahi-speaking region of Malda, in the northern part of Bengal.

In 2000 the separate state of Jharkhand was carved out of Bihar, and has absorbed some linguistic concentrations of Magahi. This is especially true in regions where dialects like

Panchpargania or Tamaria and Kurmali are spoken. Thus the Magahi region is today spread across four of India's states: Bihar, Bengal, Jharkhand, and Orissa. Our discussion in this book, however, concentrates on the dominant region of Magahi, situated in the current state of Bihar.

Magahi Folk Music and Songs

It is difficult to trace out when exactly Magahi folk songs originated. Perhaps it can be said that when human beings started settling down on the earth, songs and music started emerging. Regardless, Magahi folk songs have a very significant place in Magahi folk literature and culture as is folk songs in any other folk cultures.

One may wonder as to what makes a song folk song, as opposed to classical music. One could say that the greatest significant quality of folk music is its social relation. Classical music is a form of art music. It is related to aesthetic satisfaction in its complexities, rather than to a social function or event such as the birth of a child, sowing or reaping in agriculture, and coming of rains at different times of the year. This kind of difference also leads to other characteristics. For example, folk music has no conscious grammar, even though certain traditions can get associated with it. It may not have a consciously guided history or known authorship. Classical music, on the other hand, has more definite and inviolable structure. It is usually associated with well-established authors and creators such as Bach and Beethoven in the West and Thyagaraja and Tansen with his creation of Miyan Malhar, Miyan Sarang, and others in the Indian system. And thus we find Magahi folk songs related to such social events as the birth of a child, called *sohar*, and folk songs related to Holi, the festival of color, called *phaag*; and many others.

The Vedas tell us that folk songs have been sung for different traditional occasions across eras. Three millennia ago, the hymns of the *Rig Veda*, the earliest examples of Vedic literature, were memorized and collected. The *Rig Veda* consists of 1028 hymns composed before 1000 BC and dedicated to the gods of the Aryans (Thapar 1968); its ideas were then and are now popularly disseminated via folk songs. The songs of its traditional episodes are called *gatha* or ballads. We can observe the singing of historical *gatha* as early as the age of the *Mahabharata* by Vyasa (1000 BC), and the *Ramayana* by Valmiki (700 BC). Valmiki, for instance, writes that Lord Rama's birth was celebrated with folk songs sung by Magadhas. Lots of stories of Dushyant's son Bharata are found in the *Mahabharata*, and were also sung at that time. We find them even today in different Indian languages.

There are many other classical sources of Magahi folk songs. We can find them in the Pali Jatak, the Upanishads composed in 700 BC (Thapar 1968), and the *Brahmanas*, among others. The famous Vyasa, the creator of *Bhagavat*, has described the birth of Lord Krishna and the songs sung by beautiful women. He also tells us that Lord Krishna was often found singing with *gopis* (milkmaids) when he grew up. All these indicate that even at very ancient times folk songs were sung on pious occasions (Aryani 1975).

The great poet Kalidas (beginning of fifth century) indicates in his epic *Raghuvansh* that the village women sang praise for the King Raghu (Aryani 1975). It is said that by the third century Prakrit language had originated and folk songs had become very popular. The great poet Shree Harsh also mentioned that women sang folk songs while cultivating rice paddies.

The later Apabhransha age was also a fruitful time for folk songs. Many ballads were sung at that time also. The great poet Tulsidas described songs sung by womenfolk in the *Ramayana* (1574): At the time of Rama's wedding, the women sang abusive songs (*gaalii*), a tradition which we will see has remained particularly strong in today's Magadh. It is thus clear that the tradition of these folk songs is very ancient and had never disappeared.

There has been some academic analysis of these songs. Many Western scholars have made and translated collections of Magahi folk songs. Dr. G.A. Grierson published 'Some Bihari Folksongs' in the *Journal of the Royal Asiatic Society* (*JRAS*), which translated many Bhojpuri and Magahi songs. Grierson also published 'Songs of Alhas's Marriage' in the *Indian Antiquary*, a journal published in Bombay. There are also references to Tulsidas's *Ramayana*, Bihari's *Satsai*, Surdas's poems and Vidyapati's poetry (*Padaavali*).

A lot of Indian scholars have also made great contributions to the study of Magahi folk songs. Ram Naresh Tripathi's work is worth mentioning. Traveling widely in India, he collected numerous folk songs in different Indian languages. They appear with an introduction in *Kavita Kaumudi*, Part V, as '*Graamgeet*'. His collection presents folk songs of Uttar Pradesh and Bihar. A significant number of Magahi songs also appear in another collection of Tripathi's and are published as *sohar*, i.e. birth-related songs. His third collection, which is quite significant and is named *Hamaaraa-Graam-Saahitya*, draws primarily on the folk songs of Uttar Pradesh and provides an excellent introduction to the folk literature of that region.

A.G. Shiraz, an English civilian, also published *Hindi Folk songs*, in which there is a collection of Bihari and Magahi folk songs (Hindi Mandir 1936, Allahabad). Another scholar, Dr. Vishwanath Prasad, has edited the work *Magahi Samskar Geet*, which was published by the Patna Rashtrabhasha Parishad in 1962 and presents a collection of hundreds of Magahi folk songs. There are folk songs related to *sohar*, *mundan* (the head shaving ceremony), *janeu* (the sacred thread ceremony), and wedding and death in this work, with some discussion of the Magahi language and literature.

Dr. Sampatti Aryani, in both her doctoral dissertation and her book *Magahi Lok Sahitya*, has contributed significantly to the study of the Magahi folk literature and songs. In the introduction she devotes a critical analysis of the status of Magahi literature and presents a typology of folk tales and songs. She also devotes a chapter to Magahi riddles and proverbs. Another scholar, Ramnandan, who edited the Magahi magazine *Bihan*, has also published Magahi songs from time to time.

Now we will turn to some specific Magahi folk songs. We will begin with the *sohar* songs, which announce the birth of a child in a Magahi household and draw the women of the village to the house. The *sohar* tunes are among the most popular among the villager, but even the elite in the urban areas does not forget to sing *sohar* songs, which are *mangalik* and auspicious, when there is a new arrival in the family. These songs are joyous in nature. In some families there are no *sohar* songs if a girl is born. This may be true in a very traditional family, where a boy brings joy and a girl makes everyone in the family gloomy with the thought that her marriage will involve a lot of expenditure.

The range of Magahi *sohar* songs are diverse. Many are nursery rhymes or songs, which comprise a significant part of the folklore of every country, and which serve to fascinate children. The moon appears in a significant portion of these rhymes, and in India is represented by a child's maternal uncle, or maamoo. For example, a nursery rhyme in translation, calling the moon maamoo is as follows:

> O maternal uncle moon,
> Come here, come now and then,
> Come to the bank of the river,
> Come taking (with you) rice and
> In a golden bowl,
> And pour it at once into the
> Mouth of the baby.
>
> (P.C. Roy Choudhary, 1976)

Sohar songs make an appearance at other social functions also. For instance, the marriage ceremony in Magadh, which has social, religious and cultural importance, is also accompanied with auspicious songs throughout. The bride's people sing a particular set of joyous songs when the *Baaraat* (bridegroom's party) arrives.

Other songs are humorous and some are abusive (*gaalii* songs). One of these abusive songs reads as follows in translation:

The bridegroom is without a cap; so give him a paper cap.
The bridegroom doesn't have a pair of spectacles; offer him tin spectacles.
He does not have a shirt on his body; give him his wife's blouse.
The groom is hungry; give him cow dung to eat.
He is thirsty; give him 'nallah' (drain) water to quench his thirst.
(P.C. Roy Choudhary, 1976)

There are also more devotional songs sung while celebrating wedding rituals or when Gods are worshipped as part of a religious ritual. Then there are special *lok-geet* (folk songs) for particular festivals and *vratas*. There are seasonal *lok-geet* that are sung on different seasons. Folk songs are sung while celebrating Holi (the festival of colors) and Diwali (the festival of lights). There are *jhumar* folk songs; *barsaati* for rainy season; *birhaa*, usually sung by men, particularly *dhobis* (washermen); and *nirgun* songs, which are mystical. There are action folk songs also, such as the folk songs that are sung at the time of the transplantation of paddy or harvesting of the crops. Folk songs are widely recited and loved on religious and social occasions like Naagpanchami, Janmashtmi, Teej, Chhath and many other festivals. There are *Bahura* folk songs, usually recited by women a little before Teej festival that comes in the month of *Bhadon* (September). There are *Kajari* folk songs that are sung in the month of *Savan*.

Pastoral songs are also very popular folk songs. They express the thoughts and deep sentiments of the villagers, who may be very backward in the eyes of the educated or the literati, but who sing very popular full-throated, sentimental, thought provoking folk songs. Many of these folk songs originated at the time of the Vedas and Puranas, and continue to frame and express the daily life of an average Magahi person from birth to death.

In the course of growing up with an extended family, I came into constant contact with Magahi folk songs and music. My grandparents in particular would sing Magahi folk songs on different occasions. Frequent visits to my village would also expose me to these melodious songs. The most memorable of these songs for me was always the *gaalii* songs, which were initiated by women, educated and uneducated both, all very active. The bride's party as well as groom's party had to listen to the insult songs with their mouth shut, because they had no choice: the songs are an accepted part of the wedding celebrations. Often they would burst into laughter.

Magahi Folk Art

The history of the arts and crafts of Magadh goes all the way back to the Vedic and Upanishad period (700 BC). Excavations have revealed the unusual skill and finesse of artisans and craftsman in ancient Magadh. The folk potteries in the Kushan period around the fourth century AD and the Gupta period (319–20 BC) can be considered the zenith of these folk arts. Bronze, stone, clay, copper, silver and gold were used to create art pieces. Some of these are presented in the museum in Patna as also other museums.

Terracotta potteries of different specimens have been found in various excavations, which are unsurprising; terracotta is the medium for figurines and sculptures in many early cultures of the world. The history of terracotta figurine in Magadh started from 1000 BC, and achieved much importance in the Maurya and Gupta periods, and this art continued even in the Mughal period. Thousands of male and female figurines, animals and birds in various shapes and sizes, and various gods and goddesses made of baked clay were found among the archaeological sites of Magadh. These are excellent specimens of folk art, and were made through two processes: one process was hand-crafting, while the other was made by molding that showed off folk artists' workmanship. The terracotta artifacts reveal much to us about social life in ancient Magadh.

Bhittichitra (wall painting) is also very important folk art of Magadh, and in fact all of Bihar. Representations of Buddhist, Jaina and Sanskrit themes are very important in this form of art. The village women decorate walls of their houses with different *chitra* (painting) during the marriage ceremony or other auspicious occasions.

Kohbar painting is very famous. The *kohbar* is the room for new bride and bridegroom, and its walls are well decorated with different motifs in a beautiful manner. Usually there are four birds and a pair of geese on the wall, as well as pictures of the sun and the moon. Usually the colors are black, obtained from soot; yellow from banana leaf and milk with lime; red from flowers; and green from leaves. Recently, chemical colors have also been introduced and used.

Wall paintings are also done for *vratas* (religious observations) and *puja* (worship). There are some common symbols that appear across these kinds of wall painting: the sun and moon suggest long life; the goose and peacock are welfare; lotus flowers are calmness and goodness, and bamboos mean progeny.

Aripan or *Alpana*, or drawing on the floor, is also a stylized and very ancient folk art. It is found all over India, and appears in many famous locations, such as the Shantiniketan of Rabindranath Tagore in Calcutta. This *aripan* is drawn on the auspicious occasions of *puja*, *vratas* and on different occasions. The material which is used for this is powdered rice made into paste with water. It is drawn with fingers. Different objects, such as flowers (usually lotuses), leaves, trees, fruits, fish, peacocks, the sun, the moon, and gods are drawn. Sometimes vermilion (*sindoor*) and other coloring material are used also. Births are marked by *aripan* drawn in the *swastika* figure, which is intended to give blessings to the newly born child.

Sikki crafts are made with a kind of long grass that grows in abundance during the monsoon in Magadh areas. The village women are engaged in preparing various small articles like baskets with the upper portion of the golden stalk. Sikki grass is mixed with different colors to make different articles. Mithila is very famous for this Sikki folk art.

Magahi masks are made of dark clay found near the river banks. The mask is scrubbed, polished and painted. Many villagers are engaged in this folk art, which is frequently used in tribal dances. Particular facial expressions were painted into masks. Some of them represented gods and demons, and most are highly artistic. Ranchi areas are particularly well known for their excellent masks.

Magadh is also famous for its appliqué folk art, which has ancient roots. From Abul Fazal's book *Ain-e-Akbari* we know that *shamianas*, or colorful tents with different types of brocade patchwork, were used during times of war or for hunting. The appliqué works of Patna city and Gaya are famous and of high quality.

Kasida work is common throughout Magadh. Women embroider lots of clothing like *saris*, blouses, *kurtas*, etc. Various types of *sujni* (thick bed sheets) made of old or new clothes are still very popular all over Bihar. They are quilted with usual motifs of creepers, plants, birds, and animals, and especially different flowers. The regional clothes that are worn by men and women are very distinctive. Men wear loose shirt (*kurta*) and *dhoti*. The *dhoti* is about 4.5 yards long with less than a quarter inch wide border. *Dhotis* are generally cotton, but there are silk *dhotis* with a *zari* border (I will discuss *zari* work more later). Men often wear loose *pyjamas* also in place of *dhoti*. Women, of course, wear *saris*. *Saris* have a *pallu* at the end of it, which is embroidered heavily and is very colorful. Wedding *saris* have a *zari pallu*. Magahi women, like other Bihari women, bring the *pallu* of the *sari* in the front and tie the end of the *pallu* in their waist. This arrangement makes them look exotic and beautiful. I remember fondly that my naanii and my mother wore *saris* in that style.

The doll-making craft has been in vogue from time immemorial in all parts of Bihar. The doll is usually understood to be miniature of human figure representing actual life or character. In villages or cities the folk women made beautiful dolls of various types and sexes. They are made of bright cloths and husk and require skill. They wear *saris* and blouses, and men's clothes—*kurtas* and *dhotis*. During a wedding, these dolls are generally sent to the bridegroom's house as a token of gifts for the children of the family. Young girls learn this art of doll-making from their mother and grandmother.

They also learn the art of *mehendi*, or *henna* designs: The application of *mehendi* is used for the beautification of hands and feet during weddings or other auspicious occasions. The dark green leaves of *henna* are plucked, washed, and grounded into a thick paste with a little water. A straw needle is used for applying the paste. Beautiful designs are made in the palms, hands, and feet. The resulting stain lasts for a week or so.

Sindoor plays a very important role in the beautification of women. Married women use *sindoor* in the parting of their hair. The women apply a large round *tikaa* on their foreheads; this has become very fashionable among Indian women not only among Magahi women. Magahi village women use *sindoor* very generously and therefore look very traditional and folksy when they go about their rural activities. *Sindoor* is also used generously for religious rites, *puja* (worship) and in temples. *Pandits* apply a big *tikaa* on their foreheads while performing religious rites. *Sindoor* is a very important wedding rite all over India and not only in Magadh. This rite is mentioned in the chapter of Magahi wedding of this book.

Mahavar or *altaa* is another form of beautification. This also is used to decorate feet and toes. Court dancers used to use it also for festive occasions. Women who are not dancers use *mahavar* also. *Godana* (tattooing) is another very ancient folk art for beautification. There was a time when tattooing for a woman was very important. Today, it is getting outmoded but in villages men still get it done.

Zari work is a very important textile folk art all over India, but the *zari* work of Patna city is particularly celebrated. The work is embroidery done with gold or silver threads on satins and raw silks. Bed covers, pillowcases, caps, shoes, turbans, *saris*, carpets, etc., can all have *zari* work. Once, *zamindars*, *nawabs* and princes used to get *zari* work done on their clothing; today it is declining because of change in lifestyle and modern fashion.

The *tabak*, or gold and silver leaf, industry in Patna city was also once flourishing but has declined. This industry specialized in inlaying *tabak* (gold and silver leaves) on fine glass.

The forehead of married women used to be decorated with a shining piece of *tabak* considered the mark of fortune. This was called *tikli*. Glassy inlay work on *saris*, blouses, and turbans was another folk art.

Rangrez are professional dyers of cloth are found all over Bihar. They use their own colors and dye *saris*, etc. Wooden design blocks are for printing saris. Now they are using chemical dyes. Gaya, Patna, Bhagalpur do excellent job of dying clothes and is still flourishing.

Culinary craft in Magadh is also an established folk art. I would not say it is disappearing; it still exists to some extent, but it is not as exotic as it used to be in the past. Also different states in India have different varieties of food and today in Magadh we get different kinds of popular cuisine.

All this reminds me of my father, who also aspired to live a long life to see the world progress. His diet was driven by nutrition, though he loved home made *paneer* (Indian cheese) and *barfi* with other kinds sweets that my mother made. He indulged in clarified ghee. He ate deep fried *puris* and potato *bhujia*. For dessert he had home-made carrot *halwa* with lots of nuts, saffron, cardamoms, etc. His food was served in shiny metal *thalis* (round trays) and small *katoris* (metal bowls). Sautéed cauliflower, green *chana* (chickpeas), green peas, and green coriander *chutney* were favorite food items for him. It was a pleasing sight to watch him eat his meal. Both my father and mother lived a long life.

Magadh delicacies have a very specific taste to them. For example, Magadh people were fond of preserving fruit (*morabba*) and pickles (*achaars*). It is quite an art to save them for months. Women in particular know the art of making all kinds of lentils (*dal*), balls (*bari*) and cook them in style. The potato *bhujia* (sautéed sliced potatoes) with freshly ground *masala* (spices), especially *haldi* (turmeric) and *sarso* (mustard) paste has very typical Magahi taste. Other green vegetables, *baigan* (eggplant), *bhindi* (okra) and much more are cooked with freshly ground *masala* paste. *Dal* with fresh *haldi* paste is very tasty, and is a typical Magahi dish also. It is very popular all over India and eaten with boiled rice.

Haldi is very sacred for Magahi people. For *puja* and offerings *haldi* paste or powder is used. Basmati rice is colored yellow with *haldi* paste and offered for sacred and auspicious occasions. The *haldi* rite is one of the very important rites of Magahi wedding ceremony. I have discussed this rite in the Magahi wedding chapter of this book. *Halwa* with *haldi* paste with a lot of nuts and ghee is given to the women who have just delivered babies. It is supposed to disinfect the system of the mothers. It also gives them enough strength to be able to breastfeed their babies.

Magahi Weddings

The wedding is the most important social event for the Magahi family, and in fact, for any Hindu family. It is the sacred duty of a father to arrange for the marriage of his daughter. An astrologer predicts whether the stars of both are in harmony, and generally settles a marriage after examining the horoscopes of the bridegroom and the bride, though weddings are between families and not just individuals.

The marriage ceremony involves a number of rites, which are held in the homes of the bride and groom. The first in these wedding rites is *chhekaa. Chhekaa* is the first formality that is performed to finalize the marriage negotiation, and is falling out among more urban people. It is essentially a formalization of 'spoken for status of the would-be-bride and groom'. There is a brief ceremony first on the girl's side, which holds the boy as spoken for, which is then followed by the same kind of ceremony by the boy's side doing the same for the girl. There is token exchange of clothes, ornaments and money.

After this ceremony another very important rite is *tilak*, in which the bride and the bridegroom become formally engaged to each other. This ceremony includes various activities. The bride's father and her brother go to the house of the groom with a party consisting of selected family members and the family's priest (also called a *pandit* or *purohit*). They must get the best hospitality the groom's father can afford. They are offered sweets, tea, *paan*, cigarettes, etc., with delicacies. After the end of the meal served to the bride's father and his party, the women of the groom's family hide themselves behind a *purdah* (curtain) and sing melodious *gaalii* 'insult' songs. The men's reactions to the abuse of insult songs are good-natured. These songs are humorous and sung jokingly.

The *tilak* ends with the exchanging of engagement gifts with cash, jewelry or clothing, and the best of hospitality.

The *lagnapatri* (auspicious constellation chart) is written and an auspicious date for the wedding is fixed with the help of a *purohit* (priest). The actual wedding takes place within a short period (between one to three months) after the *tilak*, although sometimes it takes longer.

The *matkor*, or earthdigging, is a rite that takes place after the *tilak* when the bride with other women goes to a pond, river, or a well to dig earth. This earth is used in making an earthen stove (*chulhaa*) to make parched rice (a paddy called *laavaa*) for the wedding ceremony. This ceremony is *laavaa chitaaii*. Women at this time grind soaked lentils and make *baras* (deep fried lentil balls) to give them to the bride and groom during the wedding.

Ubtan, a mixture of *haldi*, mustard oil, and oatmeal flour, plays a key role in the days leading to the wedding. The women-folks in their respective homes apply it to the skin of the bride (after the *matkor*) and to the groom. *Ubtan* makes the skin delicate and shiny. The bride and the groom are blessed by the womenfolk in their respective homes after this ceremony.

During a subsequent ceremony, women perform a *chuma-avan* or 'blessing' with *haldi* in which women touch the bride's or groom's feet, knees, chest and shoulders with a stem of *duv* (grass) and bless the bride and groom. There are other rites also which are done after *haldi*. On the *haldi* day men and women participate in sprinkling turmeric on each other. It is a very joyous time and looks like a Holi event in which *haldi* water, instead of red color water, is used for play.

Two or three days before the wedding the canopy, or *mandap*, is erected in the bride's home. All the wedding's major rites are performed under the *mandap*, and a similar, smaller canopy is built in the groom's house. A *mandap* is made with colorful and beautiful red silk cloth, flowers of different colors, and shiny paper. Sometimes the four poles of the *mandap* are covered with shiny banana leaves and colored paper. The arrangements for the *baaraat* (wedding party) are made for their arrival.

On the wedding day, the groom and his party leave in a big procession, which is referred to as the *baaraat*, for the bride's home. This is meant to be a spectacular scene to announce the arrival of the groom. Band music accompanies the procession. Music, food, and drinks are very important throughout the occasion, and *shehnaai* music is traditionally played. The *shehnaai* is a double-reed horn with a very melodic horn, and famous *shehnaai* musicians are often invited to weddings. The bridegroom wears the traditional *sherwani* (a long coat up to the knees with tight trousers) of silk and brocade. He proceeds in royal fashion on a horse or a palanquin from his village. In more modern times, he rides in a very decorated car. Typically, the bridegroom's younger brother accompanies him. Many people think this signifies Rama being accompanied by his younger brother Lakshmana in his wedding, who in the *Ramayana*, are carried on a palanquin of the bridegroom and followed by a huge procession of people, music, and firecrackers. Women also follow in the initial stage as the *baaraat* leaves from the groom's house. They bless the groom with rice and betel leaves. At this time they sing happy *sohar* songs. The *baaraat* proceeds without the women and the women return to the groom's house and sing wedding songs and amuse themselves in the absence of *baaraat*.

The bride's party awaits the arrival of the groom. Diversions of various kinds take place, foods are served, and accommodations are arranged to entertain the *baaraat* party. Upon the arrival of the groom, the band leads the procession to the bride's home. The entire scene is one of great excitement. The women rejoice and get ready to greet the groom.

In *dwaar puja*, or 'worship at the door', the groom sits on his decorated horse, palanquin, or in a very fancily decorated car and, followed by a long procession of his *baaraati* with band and *shehnaai*, arrives in a very regal fashion at the bride's home. It is quite a scene to watch. Women continue to sing. The bride emerges from her house surrounded by her friends, sisters and nieces, and puts a garland over the groom's head. The groom also puts a garland over the head of the bride. The bride's mother performs a *puja* and bride's sisters give ritualized blessings. The groom returns to the *baaraat.*

Then the *vivaah*, or wedding: the ceremony itself starts with a rite called *gurhatthi.* The groom's older brother comes to the *mandap* and gives clothes and jewelry to the bride. The bride wears these clothes and jewelry to get married in the wedding ceremony. A lot of *gaalii* songs which abuse the groom's brother are sung at this occasion. After this rite the groom comes to the *mandap*. He receives a lot of clothes, which he wears in the *mandap* itself. The *purohit* starts the *havan* fire. The bride and the groom worship gods. The bride sits next to her father and the groom sits on another side for the wedding rites.

Next comes the *kanyaadaan*, or the gift of the daughter/ giving away of the bride. The father worships god and with the help of the priest he gives away his daughter. The priest places the bride's hands on her father's hand. Her mother joins them, and both the mother and the father perform the rite of *kanyaadaan*. The womenfolks sing very sad songs. The groom's father repeats Sanskrit words provided by the priest, affirming that he will accept the bride as his son's wife, and that his son will protect and support her.

The *gaanth bandhan* (knot-tying) rite follows, and represents the literal tying of the marriage knot. After *kanyaadaan* the bride sits by the groom and the ceremony of tying the marriage knot takes place. A few wedding rites are done.

The *sindoordaan*, or gift of vermilion, follows, and is a very important event in the wedding ceremony. The groom applies the vermilion to the bride's parting of the hair also in the forehead. This is a climax of the wedding, and the point at which the bride is thought to leave her home and become part of another household. The women sing sad songs because bride now 'belongs' to groom and not to her parents.

The *chumaavan* is one of the final rites of the marriage ceremony. At this stage the bride's folks (party) come to the *mandap* and bless the bride and bridegroom.. The mother of the bride puts her *sari's pallu* (end) on the head of bride and groom's, and all in attendance bless the couple with rice and flowers. The *chumaavan* is also done on other occasions, such as the *haldi* and *kohbar*.

After this bride and groom are brought to the *kohbar* room. This is the place where the bride and the groom spend their first wedding night together, and it is decorated in a very royal fashion. The *kohbar* paintings are very stylized and delicately decorated with different motifs. All the figures depict Magahi culture, and are drawn from life and nature. Usually there are birds and geese in the painting on the *kohbar* walls. There are also exotic pictures of the sun and the moon. Gentle geometric figures are produced. So, too, are human figures; a pointed nose, elongated eyes and narrow forehead characterize them. The paintings are of lotus flowers and leaves, palanquins, horses, elephants, peacocks, betel leaves, bamboos and also of deities like Ganesh, Shiva, Parvati and others. These paintings are generally done by womenfolk. The *kohbar* room is considered a very sacred place for keeping *puja* items also which are used for religious rites. *Alpana*, another form of folk art, is also generally done on the floor of *kohbar* room.

The unmarried sisters, nieces, and friends bring the bride, now newly decorated, to the *kohbar* room. They gather at the door and demand some sort of a prize or money from the groom only then they let the groom enter the room. The bride wears lots of jewelry and a heavily embroidered gold Banarasi *sari*. Her hands are colored with *mehendi* designs. Her feet and toes are colored with *altaa* (red liquid color).

After a day or so of the wedding, the *gauna*, or ceremonial departure, takes place. The girl leaves her house and goes to her *sasuraal*, or the home of her in-laws. In earlier times the bride and the groom used to be very young and the bride stayed in her own house until she grew up. Sometimes they would be 12 or 15 years old. The groom would return alone to his house. But nowadays the bride accompanies the groom, because they are both grown up, so the *gauna* takes place right after the wedding, and a *vidaai*, or formal farewell, is done. The rite of bidding formal farewell to the bride is very sad, and is accompanied by mournful singing. Women's songs are integral part of the wedding rites, and particularly of this one.

Since my father came of a large family, I have attended numerous Magahi weddings. I had lots of cousins, nephews, nieces and relatives who got married. Many weddings took place in my village Dona, near Gaya. My paternal grandfather had built a concrete mansion in the village of Dona, and the house would always be exceptionally well decorated and full of relatives for these occasions. Reaching the village was an adventure: now of course, there is a paved road to get to the village, but then, after the train would reach the station, we would travel by elephants or palanquins to the house because no buses or cars could reach it.

The preparation for the wedding would start on our arrival. We would start speaking in Magahi with each other and would hear Magahi wedding singing throughout the day. The paved courtyard of the house was huge and the provision for erecting a large colorful wedding *mandap* would be made. All ceremonies were of immense excitement, though the departure of the bride and groom followed by a lot of sad Magahi wedding songs (*sohar* songs) would make us very sad; we will return to our destination with heavy hearts.

My parents married by their mutual consent, although at that time marriage by mutual consent or by each other's liking was out of the question for most people. It was a possibility for my parents because my mother married into the same family as her older sister. My father was the younger brother of her older sister's husband. They must be visiting each other's houses when they saw and liked each other. Their wedding took place in Gaya and Dona.

My two older sisters got married arranged by my parents. Both my sisters were educated in Varanasi, at Banaras Hindu University (BHU), where they got their B.A. degrees. My eldest sister was much older than I was and I do not really remember her wedding very well. She got married in naanaa's house in Gaya by traditional Magahi rites. My middle sister Ranidi (or didi) came to Gaya after graduating. My brother-in-law (Ranidi's husband) was a magistrate and had rented naanaa's house in Gaya. Sachchanji was a very eligible bachelor and his marriage was fixed with Ranidi. Both lived close by and had seen each other, and had their marriage arranged to their liking. All the Magahi wedding rites were performed, again at my naanaa's house. I remember the *baaraat*, and how my brother-in-law came and the wedding was performed ceremoniously with songs and *shehnaai*. After the wedding Ranidi moved to her husband's house, which was very close to naanaa's house. I visited them everyday after my school.

I lived in Patna and was enrolled for a Masters in English literature in Patna College, which was a co-educational college. At that time, my parents started making arrangements for my marriage and looking for a match. I rejected quite a few matches in the beginning and my parents went along with my decisions. In an arranged marriage there are many considerations that are taken into account. The young men should ideally be of the same caste (Kayastha in this case), and should have a decent job and earn enough money for a good looking educated girl of a good family. My parents heard of a young man who was good looking and with a Masters in English literature from Patna College itself where I was studying. He came from a good family. They met with him and approved him for marriage with me. That young man, Manindra, who did become my husband, had completed his education at that college just when I joined it, and therefore I had not seen him. But I did hear a lot about him in the student Common Room of Patna College. People knew him and he seemed to be very popular. The professor who taught me had also taught him, and seemed to hold a high opinion of him as well.

The *tilak* ceremony for us took place with the same rituals and ceremonies that I described earlier. The priest, of course, had matched our horoscopes, before the arrangement was settled. The dates for the wedding and other related rituals were then agreed upon by both sides and announced. The list of relatives and invitees included some of our common professors. This projected marriage was quite an arranged marriage; I did not meet him until our wedding day. My brother Rajiva Ranjan was posted in Patna as a magistrate at that time. He knew Manindra well. He also said favorable things about him, which helped me avoid whatever anxiety I had about this arranged marriage. I was quiet and agreeable. I don't know why I did not express my desire to see Manindra.

My wedding was in Patna, and it involved a lot of work. We had to arrange many pre-wedding ceremonies. Like all mothers, my mother had started collecting clothes and jewelry. I was sent to Calcutta to shop for clothes and jewelry. The items I purchased are still with me, and I still like them. Tailors, embroiderers, coppersmiths, goldsmiths, and dyers arrived at our home. The confectioners came with their large vessels, and made mountains of sweets. Arrangements had to be made for feeding the relatives and guests. Lots of my relatives lived in Patna itself, and joined us to attend all the Magahi rituals and ceremonies. Those relatives who lived in Patna went to their own houses to sleep at nighttime and came to my house in the morning, but those friends and relatives who were from out of town stayed with us for a week or more. All the arrangements were made for their stay. Each evening, they would gather in the larger courtyard and sing Magahi *sohar* songs with the *dholki* (an oblong drum). Until late into the night, the beat of the *dholki* and the singing continued while I, the bride sat in the corner in a reverie. These songs seemed to reassure me. The girls drew designs on my hands and feet with henna and used the *henna* paste to decorate their own hands also. The last two days were full of excitement and I forgot my anxiety. I still had not seen the bridegroom. Early in on the wedding morning, men and workers came to make the *mandap*, a pavilion of leaves and flowers in which the wedding ceremony would take place that night. Banana plants were the pillars of the *mandap* and a colorful top covering was made with mango and banana leaves and a red *chandni* of silk cloth. Inside the pavilion was also decorated with flowers and colorful paper chains, garlands, and ribbons.

The evening arrived; it was the time to prepare for the wedding. I had not bathed or changed clothes for two days. Women had applied a lot of *haldi* paste with oat flour paste (*ubtan*) to make my skin glowing and delicate. I bathed with the ritual water, which was saved from a *puja*. And after this the women became busy with the fun task of making up and dressing up the bride. They used a lot of perfume; they tied my hair up into a high bun with white jasmine flowers and gold chains; and they dyed my hands and feet with red color. My hands were covered in *henna* designs; my face, eyes, and lips were all appropriately made up, lipsticked, and kajaled. I was dressed in a gold tissue silk *sari* and decorated with lots of jewelry from head to toe.

The *baaraat* arrived at the door for *jaymala* (garland). A lot of *shehnaai* music accompanied with other instruments were being played. The women of my side also were singing loudly while holding their ritual *thali* (silver plate) to begin the rituals. The bridegroom stepped out of his highly decorated car with flowers, ribbons, and balloons. We exchanged *jaymala*. The girls at my side and I were very anxious to see the bridegroom, but we could not. He was dressed in a silk *shervani* and *churidar pyjama* with a glittering *maur* on his head. After the ceremony, the bridegroom went back to be in the *baaraat*, and I was brought inside also.

For the wedding ceremony, I changed into a red *sari* with gold ornamentation called *chunderi*. The rituals required I should bathe again with the *puja* water, which was saved for me, but I refused to do so—I was all made up and dressed up, and I didn't want to do the same thing again. The wedding ceremonies went on until late night and I was wedded with all the appropriate Magahi rituals. My parting of the hair was full of *sindoor*. I wore my red *chunderi sari* loaded with jewelry.

The night became hectic. I was led to a very decorated *kohbar* room. Young girls and ladies surrounded me. They sat and chatted with the groom for a while. Women looked. at the bride and groom with admiration. I still had not seen the bridegroom and was anxious to know what he looked like. My anxiety and worry got intense. I was experiencing a lot of suspense. The girls and women all left the room. I raised my mantle and looked up. We started conversing and chatting with each other. Time passed quickly and my worry had disappeared. I uttered to myself, 'not bad'.

It became morning. The bridegroom was led to a different room. My parents, sisters, and brothers were all at the door of my room. They probably saw peace on my face and felt relieved. A couple of days went by and the time had come for my departure to my *sasuraal*. My parents had a hard time saying good-bye to their beloved daughter. I was helped to a decorated car in which the groom also sat. I arrived my in-laws' house. The house was huge with lots of people. By this time my fear had gone. I went through a lot of rituals once again. My in-laws, Manindra's brothers, sisters, guests and relatives greeted me with great affection, speaking in a Bhojpuri language. I had not heard this dialect of Bhojpuri before and fell in love with it right away.

The last wedding which I attended in India (Patna) was that of my brother's. He was older than me and had not gotten married. He had difficulty finding a girl of his choice. When he finally found one and got married, this too was of course an arranged marriage.

Magahi Fairs and Festivals

Magahi fairs and festivals are important factors that influence the social and daily life in Magadh villages and cities. The Magahi areas have a large numbers of festivals and *melaas* (fairs). These *melaas* attract large numbers of people. People participate in these *melaas* when the crops are harvested. Magahi festivals and *melaas* are important religious festivals that attract huge crowds. In this chapter, I will begin by describing several major festivals in detail, and then I will turn to several smaller festivals. Finally, I will relate some of my own experiences with Magahi fairs and festivals.

Different festivals are observed and different folk songs are sung at different points in the year. Makar Sankranti or Tilsankranti is observed in Magadh, as well as all over India. It falls on the 14th of January (*Maagh*). The god Indra is thanked for providing rain for the generous growth of crops, while Surya (sun) is thanked for providing sunshine for the growth of crops. Poor people are given charity on this day. The day starts with a massage with *til* (sesame) oil and thereafter a dip in the holy water. Special food is prepared for this day. Beaten rice, rice flakes, *chuuRaa*, curds, and sesame sweets with brown sugar are very popular.

On solar eclipse days most Magahi people bathe and do prayers. During the eclipse the sun is believed to be combating with demon Rahu. Prayers are made for the sun's success, and when the sun has freed himself from the grasp of the demon and sheds his full luster on the earth, people bathe and offer alms to Brahmins.

In the month of *Maagh* (late January) Vasant Panchami takes place. Saraswati, the goddess of wisdom and learning is worshipped all over Magadh on this day. It is also called Saraswati Puja. On this day, people wear yellow clothes, they dye clothes in turmeric paste and water. The idol of Saraswati is profusely decorated with yellow flowers and yellow sweets, primarily at schools and educational institutions. Special sweets are saffron *halwa* and chickpea flour *laddu*. Other items put before the idol are new books, blank paper, pen, and musical instruments. Saraswati grants blessings to obtain learning, wisdom and musical talents. After the worship is over, the clay image is taken out in a procession and immersed in the river.

The festival of Shivaratri is also celebrated with rejoicing and feasting. Shivaratri literally means the night of Shiva. The story is that this is the night when Shiva appeared in human form. In reality Shiva is the name of the almighty god who is formless, and who is also called Shambhu and Shankar.

Holi, the festival of color, is one of the important festivals. It is observed in the month of *Faalgun* (March). It is also called 'Phaag' or 'Phagua'. The songs that are sung on this occasion are called Holi also. There are various legends current among the Magahi people and other people regarding the origin of the Holi festival. The important one is as follows:

In ancient times there lived a demoness named Holika who preyed upon children. This brought great misery to the people. People went to Saint Vashishtha, the preceptor of Rama, and asked for his help. He told them to light a pyre for Holika that could consume the demoness. The people accordingly lighted a huge fire and the demoness was driven to it. She was reduced to ashes and people were saved.

Another version of the story is as follows:

A demon named Hiraniaksha had a sister named Holika and son named Prahlaad. Hiraniaksha hated Rama, while his son Prahlaad was a great devotee of Rama. At last, the demon decided to kill his son. He entrusted his sister with the mission to kill his son. Holika raised a big pile of cow-dung cakes and set it on fire. She sat on the pile with Prahlaad in her lap. Through the grace of Rama, Prahlaad remained uninjured while Holika was reduced to ashes. Today, the offerings thrown into fire consist of sweets and fruits. It is believed that people who worship the Holi fire are blessed with long life, prosperity and wealth. The celebration of Holi is the celebration of victory over evil. Although Holi falls on the full moon day of *Faalgun*, the rejoicing starts much earlier. The rejoicing consists of mostly playing with colored water, although some people indulge in indecent and *gaalii* songs.

Another aspect of the celebration is *Holika Dahan*, or Holi fire, dust play:

Holi fire is celebrated the night preceding the Holi day. In Magahi country this Holi fire is also known as 'burning the year'. According to the Indian system the year begins with the Holi day, and therefore the preceding night is burning the preceding year. Quite often incense materials are put in this fire during an auspicious hour that is supposed to spread fragrance and cleanse the atmosphere. With the dust created by this Holi burning young people indulge in a kind of dust play among them with colored powder or colored water and even mud mixed in the dust. More commonly in Magahi country, later in the day only colored powder is used without any dust after men and women have taken a shower and put on fresh and new clothes. There is also a tradition of singing Holi songs in groups. Groups of people go from house to house singing Holi songs. The instrumental accompaniments are relatively simple, consisting essentially of a drum called *dholak* and different kinds of cymbals and tambourines called *jhaal* and *kartaal*.

Rama Navami falls in *Chaitra* (March). It marks the auspicious day when Lord Rama was born, and is observed both in Bihar and across India. People celebrate it by observing fasts and offering prayers in his honor. The festival Krishna-Janmashtami or Janmashtami, in the month of *Bhado* (August), is a popular festival celebrating Lord Krishna's birth. People fast and offer prayers. Navaratri, Vijaydashami/Dussehra are festivals that involve the worship of Devi Durgaa and Lord Rama. They are celebrated all over India. Durgaa Puja is a very important festival in Bihar and Bengal. The goddess Durgaa symbolizes Shakti, the physical, moral and spiritual power of the female, while Lord Rama is the human incarnation of God. A very beautiful and large clay image of goddess Durgaa is made and is profusely decorated for the Durgaa Puja, and the entire cities of Gaya and Patna, where I spend most of my childhood, would shine with the decorations for the festival.

The festival of Dussehra is celebrated for ten days by enacting scenes from the life of Rama as depicted in the *Ramayana*. The activity of enacting these scenes is called Rama Leela, and involves processions and fairs that form over the course of these ten days. As children, we would participate in all these activities—schools and colleges would close for a month or so. People would line up the street on both sides to have a glimpse of Lord Rama's idol, and would throw flower petals at the idol in reverence. Many devotees would fast for nine days. The tenth day was the climax of the festival, when the monstrous sized effigies of the demon Raavana were set on fire. A celebration would be held to depict the destruction of Raavana and victory of Lord Rama, and at the end of the tenth day an image of Durgaa is taken to the nearest river and immersed in water. This immersion is called *visarjan*.

Another very important festival is Diwali, the festival of lights. Diwali is the Hindi word for the Sanskrit 'Dipaavali', which literally means rows of lights. It is celebrated in the month of *Kartika* of the Indian lunar calendar, which generally falls some time during the month of October. On this day every house is cleaned thoroughly and decorated with rows of lights (*diyaa*) in interesting patterns. Tradition has it that it was on this day that Lord Rama returned home to Ayodhya after defeating Raavana in Lanka, and that his return was greeted with a festival of lights. Merchants celebrate this day by worshipping Lakshmi, the goddess of wealth. It starts a new business year for them.

When I was a child, we would go around to look at the well-lit city as the lights glittered. I very clearly remember lighting firecrackers in celebration. I also celebrate Diwali in the United States, where I reside now. We don't light earthen *diyaa* (lamp) here as we did in India, but candles glitter equally well.

Godhan comes a couple of days after Diwali. It is a very Magahi festival. It is supposed to be performed by sisters for the welfare of their brothers. On that day sisters tie *raakhee* (amulets) on their brothers' wrists. Brothers treat their sisters well in some way, generally by giving them some money as a token of protection. The word *raakhee* comes from *rakshaa*, and the full name of the amulet is *rakshaa bandhan*, a protection tie. The idea behind the festival is that, with the tying of the *raakhee*, a brother undertakes the responsibility of protection and welfare of his sister. Women may tie this *raakhee* on a man's wrist in order to mark him as a substitute brother and to qualify for his protection.

We now briefly turn to some other festivals. There is a festival called Daawaat Puja observed by Magahi people. Some Magahi children begin reading and writing for the first time on this day. The Kayastha caste people also celebrate Chitragupta Puja. Naag Panchami is a festival observed on the fifth day of the bright half of *Savan* (July–August). On Naag Panchami, *pujas* are done honoring snakes and serpents, as they are considered gods also. The story of this festival is as follows:

One day, an affluent farmer's plough killed three serpent babies. The mother serpent became very angry because of this and bit everyone in the farmer's house, except for the farmer's married daughter, who was at her in-laws' home. The serpent went to her in-law's house to bite her. The daughter knew the story of the death of her family, and she brought a bowl of milk with parched rice and put it in front of the serpent. She began to ask forgiveness. The female serpent was very pleased with the daughter—she blessed the farmer's daughter and told her she could request a boon from the serpent. The farmer's daughter asked that her family be brought back to life. The serpent granted her wish on that day (which was *panchami*), and from then on, Naag Panchami is celebrated so that those who worship *naag* and *naagin* (the male and female serpent) might also be granted protection from snakes.

There are also important festivals called Teej and Jiutia, which fall in the months of August and September. Married women observe Teej by praying for the long lives of their husbands. On this day, women distribute lots of *perakias* (homemade sweets) to their neighbors and relatives. Jiutia, on the other hand, is observed for the long lives of sons and daughters, but more so for sons. I provide some interesting Teej and Jiutia stories in my ballad folk tale chapter.

ChhaTha is another very important *vrata* (observance) for Magahi people, although it is also observed all over Bihar. ChhaTha is a 'surya *vrata*', or sun observance, and is important because the sun is believed to be both the visible manifestation of the almighty god, as well as the observer of things—nothing escapes his notice. The story of ChhaTha is detailed in my ballad and folk tale section; here, I will discuss the *vrata*, which is primarily performed by women. Women who perform the *vrata* believe that a vow made to the sun is a sure way to attain their desires. Their vows are chiefly made with the object of securing a son, but they make other wishes, as well. If their desire for a son is fulfilled, then these women sometimes name their son after the sun god, Surya. Unmarried girls make vows to the sun in order to attain *akhand saubhagya*, or eternal exemption from widowhood. Cultivators are said to observe vows in honor of the sun for the safety of their cattle.

The *arghya* plays an important part in ChhaTha observances. It is an offering of water, rice and flowers to the sun, and is done every morning when the sun rises. It is said this offering can bring prosperity, children and welfare for husbands. It is also said to cure people suffering from disorders of eyes, barrenness in women, and other physical disorders. The *arghya* is offered every morning at sunrise. *Aditya hridaya-path* is the prescribed *mantra* for sun worship, while the 'Gayatri' is the most sacred *mantra* in honor of the sun.

The Bihari Hindus who observe the festival of ChhaTha eat basmati rice, dal and squash curry on that day. On the following day the women fast during the day and in the night they eat *khiir*, pudding made with basmati rice, thickened milk and sugar. On the next day they offer *arghya* (offerings) to the sun god. The offerings are fruits and *thekua*, which are made in bulk. They are also called *khurma*. In the morning again, offerings are made to the rising sun by the side of the holy river Ganga, or any other river. The entire city shows up on the *ghaat* (shore) of the Ganga. Beautiful, colorful *saris* and clothes glitter by the side of the water in the sunshine as they offer their prayers to the sun. The hundreds of people who participate in the *puja* receive offerings of *thekua* and sing melodious *chhatha* folk songs. It is quite a sight to watch.

My mother used to observe this *vrata* with fasting. All of our relatives, friends would assemble by the Ganga's banks in Patna and share the delicious *thekua*. *Thekua* are made of wheat flour, and as I think they may delight readers, I have provided a recipe below:

4 cups of wheat flour
1 cup of molasses or brown sugar
Ghee to deep-fry *thekuas*
1 cup of whole milk
1 tsp of aniseed (optional)
1 cup of ghee for the wheat dough

Mix all the ingredients well and make smooth dough. Divide the dough into large balls. Roll the dough out thickly on a cutting board and cut them into round shapes with a large cookie cutter. Deep-fry the cookie-shaped *thekuas* in ghee. They should come out golden brown in color.

Although there are not many temples for sun worship in Bihar (there is one in Saharsa district, and the most famous one is in Deo, Gaya district), the temples that do exist celebrate the ChhaTha ceremony on a very large scale on the third day of the month *Kartik* (October–November).

These religious festivals come with *melaas* and fairs, and which would attract thousands of people, Magahi people among them. Rama Navami attracts a big crowd, as do Vijaydashami/Dussehra, Holi and Diwali. Torches, bicycles, shoes, and various toiletries always sold very well at these *melaas*. Even the village women in *purdaa* would come to these *melaas* to buy things.

The Sonepur *melaa* is a particularly famous fair. It has an ancient tradition and is closely associated with Harihar Nath temple at Sonepur, and is known as a particularly prosperous and well-visited *melaa* throughout Bihar. People went to the extent of saying that it is the world's best *melaa* for the cattle business. Numerous kinds of animals were sold in this *melaa*, such as bullocks, cows and horses and even sheep, mules, and elephants. While healthy bullocks and cows came from the Punjab and the sheep from the far north, horses came from such distant places as Kabul.

This *melaa* also attracted tradesmen from all over the country. People from the cities of Calcutta, Allahabad, and Lucknow, among others, would bring goods for display and sale. Europeans came to deal in jewelry, cutlery, hardware, crockery, furniture, and leather goods. English goods were brought for sale. English tailors would come from Calcutta to make suits. Nepalese and Tibetan artisans would also join in the display of their products. Regional specialties, such as brass and silver curious from Orissa, were also available at the Sonepur *melaa*, as were cottage industries goods like *durries* (handmade carpets), glazed potteries, and artistic stoneware from Gaya. There are also various kinds of song and dance entertainments available at such fairs. I have a good recollection of the Sonepur *melaa*, which I would attend with lots of our friends. We would ride in boats and enjoy our visit and participation in other ways.

I was also fond of the *melaas* in the Gaya district, where I was born and raised. Gaya is a very ancient city sacred to both the Hindus and the Buddhists, and most *melaas* in Gaya are religious, centering on famous temples. In Gaya, the full moon day 'Purnima' of the month of *Baisakh* (April–May) is very important for the Buddhists: this was the day when Lord Buddha was born, attained enlightenment and ascension. A big *melaa* is held at Bodh Gaya where the famous Buddhist temple is situated. The sacred scriptures of Buddhists are cited. The *melaa* is highlighted by cultural shows and art exhibitions, and by the buying and selling of agricultural tools, handicrafts, cattle and art products. The celebration in 1956 to mark the 2500th year of Lord Buddha's ascension attracted thousands of pilgrims from all over the world.

As I was born and had spent my childhood in Gaya, I participated in these activities with my grandparents. They would go to Bodh Gaya quite frequently. The whole atmosphere of Bodh Gaya was very serene, and we loved to spend time there. My grandparents and also my parents were staunch theosophists. They believed in Anne Besant's and Krishnamurti's preaching, and attended conferences and convocations every year. My grandfather was also very much influenced by Lord Buddha's preaching. He lived in Gaya and Bodh Gaya until his end. Both my grandparents died in Patna.

The Evil Eye and Other Superstitions in Magahi

The belief in the evil eye is not simply Indian, but is held by people all over the world. This belief in the evil eye is quite common in India, and is recognized in the sacred books of Hinduism. The general idea is as follows: some evil is transferred from one person to another, often with evil intentions, but not always. A look of admiration can also harm the victim. It may not be possible for the person to realize when the evil eye affected him or her. Most of the time it affects children or younger ones. It also sometimes affects domestic animals. A lot of precaution should be taken to avoid evil influences, which can be inflicted during the time of marriage, childbirth and puberty.

In his book *The Evil Eye* (1992) Alan Dundes describes how he was thanked by an American woman, married to a man (from Yugoslavia), because she finally understood why her parents-in-law never complimented her or praised her children, no matter what she did to impress them. The children also never received any words of praise from their grandparents. After she heard Alan Dundes's lecture, things became clear. She realized that her in-laws belonged to an evil eye culture. What she had mistaken as a 'personal affront for many years was nothing more than culture-bound caution' (Dundes 1992: ix).

As Dundes points out in his book, the evil eye is not an old-fashioned superstitious belief as many people think. It is a strong ethos that affects the people throughout the Indo-European and Semitic world. In India, in the Arab world, in the Mediterranean, and in South America and North America one will find people who believe in the effect of the evil eye.

Evil eye means ill effects of praise. Infants, children and young adults are very susceptible to the evil eye. A lot of care is taken to guard against exposure to it. Greek mothers, for instance, can refuse to show the children even to their fathers. The Greek mothers are guarded against compliments given to them or to the newly born babies. Turkish women are happy when the new arrival is totally ignored because this spares the risk of having the evil eye cast upon it. I have read about a Scottish woman who got scared by a complimentary remark given to her cute baby. She immediately turned her child's face and began to spit on it as hard as she could. The Rabbis of Palestine advised to call a beautiful baby 'ugly darky'. The Chinese call their children 'dog', 'hog', 'puppy', etc., to guard against their young children from the evil eye (Dundes, 1992).

The evil eye, it is believed, comes out of jealousy. Magahi people, like people all over India, believe in *nazar*, which means 'evil eye', most specifically the malign cast of envy. It can inflict its power to destroy almost anything. For instance, a woman who has no children admires another woman with beautiful children. She can invoke jealousy or envy and cause harm to the children. Alternatively, a person with physical defects who happens to see someone blessed with healthy physical condition is believed to certainly have a sense of malice or envy towards the healthy person.

Magahi people are no exception as far as the evil eye belief is concerned. In Magadh, it is believed that women, rarely men, and sometimes also deities, commonly cast that evil eye. The planet Shani (Saturn), for example, is notorious for the burning gaze of his evil eye. A few animals are possessors of the evil eye also, but the superstitious dread of an evil eye seems to come mostly from women in the Magahi tradition. If a boy were to fall sick one will hear words like, 'Sonu (the boy's name) was playing in the neighborhood with other boys wearing a pretty outfit and was chirping a lot when that devilish woman came and her *nazar* fell on him', or 'the little girl was eating a delicious dish when the devilish woman came and cast her an evil eye. The girl vomited whatever she ate because of the evil *nazar*.'

It is very interesting to note that they take precautions against the evil eye the same way as people of other parts of the world do. Many people, especially women, smear lamp black (called *kajal*) on their eyes to avoid the evil eye. Children are also smeared with dots of lamp black to save them from evil influences. There are other ways by which persons may immunize themselves from evil influence. During the prenatal period the mother is subject to various taboos so that evil spirits may not victimize her. She observes a lot of restraints. During the eclipse she is not supposed to sleep in an open courtyard or under a tree. She has to wear amulets to ward off the evil eye. Amulets are also used to cure diseases. They are made of gold, silver, copper and iron. They are tied to the forearm with black silk thread. A pregnant woman must also take much care so that she does not see objects that can cause evil influence; they may affect her child. In certain negative circumstances a father must not look at his newly born child until a favorable time and then he must see only its reflection in a *thali* (metal tray) of oil. Putting black mark on an infant's cheek to divert the evil eye may protect him. Mothers will try to make the faces of their children ugly by painting black marks on the cheeks, forehead or chin so that the children are not influenced by the admiring glances of evil eye.

Beyond people and animals, the power of evil eye also influences buildings, garden, and crops. If a beautiful building is admired it may be spoiled. Carpenters and builders are in constant dread of evil eye; they leave the buildings unfinished to avoid the effect of evil eye. Farmers also do many things to save their crops from evil eye. Other customary practices to guard against the evil eye include pouring a few drops of milk with a fig or betel leaf on the foreheads of a couple during marriage. An alleviatory measure for the mother or some relative of the child suffering from the effects of the evil eye is to put mustard seeds, salt and chilies in a cup, and to pass it three times around the child's head and puts into fire. This is believed to cure the child.

There are also various superstitious beliefs that people believe regarding omens. If when leaving the house on a visit or with a mission, a black cat crosses one's path it is considered a bad omen. If on leaving the house, a man sees a woman with a pitcher filled with water on her head, it indicates the mission will be complete. When crows crow on the roof of the house, it indicates an arrival of a guest or a relative. The throbbing of a right eye of a man and left eye of a woman is good omen but the opposite is bad. If a dog or a cat cries in front of the house, it is considered bad omen. A washer man carrying washed clothes is lucky omen. A corpse on the street, and the sight of fish, or of curd are good and auspicious omens.

Some numbers are believed to be auspicious and some inauspicious. A belief exists that if a mission is started with three people it is bound to fail. This is underscored by the Magahi proverb *teen tikat maha vikat*, which means, three people going on a mission is a dangerous thing. The number 5 and 7 are believed to be auspicious, and at the start of a mission five or seven betel nuts are given to the adventurer. This number of betel nuts is also used for many ceremonies.

Certain days of the week are considered lucky, while other days are considered unlucky. Monday, Wednesday, Thursday and Friday are lucky, while Tuesday, Saturday and Sunday are not so lucky days. It is common belief that one should not go in certain directions on certain days. It can result in *dishaa-shuul*, or opposition caused by direction. There are auspicious days for sending a girl to her husband's house. They are Monday, Thursday or Friday but not Tuesday or Saturday. It is not good to eat *bhuujaa* (roasted gram) and *khichari* (a dish with the mixture of rice and dal or split peas) on Sundays, as the person who eats it will become poor. If, however, he eats these on Saturday, he will be blessed.

Some of the Hindu holidays are considered auspicious for performing certain deeds while inauspicious for performing other deeds. Certain colors are thought to have protective value. For instance, red, blue, and turmeric (yellow) are good and auspicious. Black is not auspicious and should not be used for any good occasions. White is associated with death; widows wear it.

There are superstitious beliefs entertained by people regarding sneezing. It is a very common Magahi belief that if someone sneezes before a person who is about to begin an auspicious deed, like performing a marriage ceremony or any sacred deed, or like going on trips for some mission, the performer should halt for a while after the sneeze. There is the fear that the work or mission will not be complete. If the sneeze is repeated, however, then no harm is caused.

Other superstitions concern food. Doors should be closed while eating; otherwise, hungry men may look in. If someone is eating outdoors in an open field and another passes, the eater should offer the passerby food. In one traditional tale, a man who was eating sweets and refused to give it to another person got sick. The sickness was cured only when sweets and coconuts were offered to the goddess.

The evil eye can be turned away and it can be cured, it is believed. Magic and sorcery act as rites and practices to counteract the evil effect. After death, also, many things are done to the dead body so that his soul goes to the heaven. The *shraaddha* ceremony is well known all over India. Attempts are made by many ways to divert evil influence that may cause harm to the dead.

I grew up in Magahi surroundings trying to avoid evil eye effects. When I was three of four years old, I used to play in the courtyard with a lot of children. When I used to come home my maternal grandmother (naanii) would smear lampblack *kajal* on my eyelids to save me from evil eye. Naanii also used to take a handful of red dry chilies, salt and mustard seeds which she would pass around my face and throw into fire to avert the influence of evil eye.

I reside in America now and feel like 'touching wood' when a praise is inflicted upon little ones. This custom is American, not Indian or Magahi. On the other hand, I want little ones to wear a lot of *kajal* in their eyes to avoid evil spirits. Superstition seems to be ingrained in me. My naanii used to smear *kajal* on my eyelids to save me from evil eye. Even now when I reside in the USA, I am careful about evil influence. I eat fish and yogurt when I go on fruitful trips. If a black cat crosses my path when I am driving, I somehow try to stop the car for a while if I can. As the product of an evil-eye culture, I cannot avoid taking precautions against bad omens.

Birth, Death and Reincarnation

As I noted earlier in my discussion of folk music and songs, the birth of a child in a Magahi family is treated as a major event and characterized by a traditional celebration. Before the actual birth, the pregnant woman observes certain rites. It is believed that, if a pregnant woman's wishes are not fully met, her child may go through life in a somewhat dissatisfied manner. *Sohar* singing begins the moment a child is born, and is supposed to grant the child an auspicious beginning. The rest of the birth ceremony begins even before the umbilical cord is cut, with the whispering of some sacred *mantras* (spells) in the baby's ears while placing a mixture of honey and ghee in his mouth. As soon as women of the neighborhood friends and relatives hear about the childbirth, they assemble and join in the singing of the *sohar*, often accompanied by the *dholak*. These various sanctifying rites (*samskaara*) are observed differently depending on the timing of the child's birth.

At the particular moment when the child is born and his umbilical cord is cut, those in attendance sing the sweetest songs. When the child is born and when his umbilical cord is cut at that particular time sweet tunes of songs are sung. On that occasion, ancestors are told through prayer songs that their family successor has been born, and the holy ancestors bless the child. Gold articles, such as bowls, are used to heighten the auspiciousness of the moment. Magahi Muslims also participate in singing *sohar*, although most of the songs mention Lord Rama's birth.

There are celebrations following the day of birth. Many of these ceremonies are rarely practiced in their full form, even in orthodox families. The sixth day after the birth is *chhathii.*

The twelfth day is *baarahvi.* On the twentieth day following the birth *bisauri* is observed, when both mother and child are considered pure after a sacred bath and *puja.* They are exposed to the rays of the sun, and the child wears amulets of gold or copper to ward off evil spirits. If the child's birth falls under an inauspicious constellation then the *bisauri puja* is done on the twenty-seventh day and called *sataisaa.*

The twenty-seventh also marks the first time a father can see his baby son for the first time. He is prohibited from seeing his child until that time, when he sees his son for the first time in a metal plate full of oil. *Sohar* songs are sung continuously at this time.

The naming ceremony, or *naamkaran*, is held on the twelfth day after the childbirth, provided he is not born in the *sataisaa* period. The first feeding ceremony, *annaprashana*, is even more important than the naming ceremony. In its sixth month, the child is given rice mixed with curds, honey and ghee.

As for the gender of the infant, from the earliest hymns of the *Rig Veda* sons were looked on as great blessings. One son, at least, was almost essential to perform funeral rites for his father, and thus ensure his safe transit to the other world. The intense family feeling of Hindus enhanced the desire for sons: without them the line would disappear. In the best Magahi families, however, girls were called for and liked just as much as sons.

The general impression obtained from the literature is that, in ancient India, the child's life after infancy was a happy one. The small child in ancient India was generally pampered, humored and allowed freedom, privileges which few children in Europe obtained until modern times.

After infancy, the Magahi child's major *samskaara* is the first shaving of the child's head. This is called *mundan*, and includes an *upanayan*, or sacred thread ceremony. *Upanayan* is also called *janeu* in some regions and homes. The boy is given *yagnopavita* (sacred thread) before an audience of priests, relatives and friends. In some families a *mandap* (canopy), where the rituals take place, is erected in front of the house and decorated with banana and mango leaves. Priests and barbers get gifts of cloth, money and grains.

One of the religious duties of a son in the Magahi family is to perform the last rites of the deceased father for his spiritual salvation. The dead body carried on bier by four persons is cremated on the bank of a river. The eldest son of the deceased person was the main *karta*—he undertakes all the funeral rites, and he is the chief mourner. The main *shraaddha* is performed on the twelfth day after the death of the deceased. *Tarpan* and *pinda*, oblation and balls of rice, are offered to the deceased by the *karta*. The family priest utters *mantras* for the salvation of the soul. Generally, the *shraaddha* is performed according to the means of the family, sometimes people try to do it very generously and go beyond their means. *Shraaddha* is also done in Gaya at a later date.

The dead body of a child aged six and eight years is often buried, not cremated.

The spirits of the deceased receive systematic worship when *shraaddha* or funeral ceremonies are performed on anniversary of the death. Such holy performance takes place in Gaya and other places also. At this occasion *pitriyas* (deceased ancestors) are worshipped on the thirteenth or fourteenth day of the dark half of *Savan*. It is said that *purvajas* or ancestral spirits descend to the levels of ghosts when they are strongly attached to worldly objects. It is said that such spirits possess the bodies of their descendants. Adequate *shraaddha* ceremonies are performed for their release. Brahmins are feasted. Water is poured at the root of the *peepal* tree; *tarpan* or offerings of *pinda* of rice balls are offered to the deceased.

Of all the days of the *shraaddhian*, the 13th, 14th and 15th are considered to be of special importance. The *pitriyas* are also worshipped on auspicious occasions, especially on the occasion of marriages. It is also believed that if feasts are given to the relatives of the deceased and to Brahmins the *pitriyas* are satisfied. The soul does not perish unless it merges into divine self and achieves *moksha* or salvation. The desires of a man who is dying do not allow his soul to ascend beyond a certain stage. He remains as a ghost (*bhoot*) until his soul is purified from the sins he has committed by performing the right funeral ceremonies. For relieving ancestral spirits from their low order of *bhoots*, *shraaddhas* are performed by their relatives in a holy place like Gaya and other similar cities. People who die with selfish and wicked thoughts present in them descend in the world as evil spirits. Their wishes are unfulfilled, and adequate *shraaddhas* rites are performed to satisfy them, which also eliminates from wicked thoughts.

In the Magahi world-view, God rewards good deeds and punishes evil ones. If a person has not been punished for all his evil deeds in the present life, his soul, after his death, will carry the account to his next birth, when he will be accountable for what he did in his past life. His deeds are called *karma*. The cycle of births continues because of his *karma* (actions). The goal of a person is to get out of this cycle by continuously doing selfless deeds and asking god to grant him liberation from the cycle (*samsaara*). When this happens, the individual merges his identity (*samskaara*) in the supreme soul.

God gives us life, sustains us, and when the time comes, absorbs us back either into himself or sends us back to the earth into new life, all in accordance with our *karma*. The term *karma* was first mentioned in Vedic *Brahmanas* (900 BC) It tells us about ritual actions about performing sacrifices, offerings and gifts to gods. *Karma* means action that causes good results (Pandharipande 1990). Pandharipande rightly points out that the concepts of *karma* and *dharma* (duty toward society or yourself) had a great impact on how people lived their lives. All actions bring results (*phal*), and the present life and situation are the result of actions performed in the past. Therefore, in the same way, all the actions performed in the present will have consequences for the future life.

The results of the action will not have effects in the present life. In order to experience results, a man will have to be reborn. Naturally, this brings us to the theory of rebirth. Good actions bring good results and bad results bring bad actions, just as good seeds produce good plants and bad seeds produce bad plants. Right and wrong actions do not simply affect one life, but also have effects on other lives also.

Karma also justifies the four classifications of the society. These four classifications of society are Brahman, Kshatriya, Vaishya and Shudra. The *Upanishad* (5:10:7) says that one who performs good acts is born in the Brahman, Kshatriya or Vaishya class, but one who does not perform right action is born as a Shudra, or a dog or a pig. Good *karma* offers hope for the betterment of one's life: if a better quality of life does not come with this birth it certainly will in different births. Thus one should accept his present life and treat it as an opportunity to improve his future lives. Exactly how we determine right or wrong actions is a valid question that can be answered by *dharma*.

Both of India's great epic poems, the *Ramayana* and the *Mahabharata*, discuss the conflict of *karma* and *dharma*. The *Ramayana* reflects people and society as ideals, and it conveys the role of the supernatural and *karma* in human destiny, but the *Mahabharata* portrays people and society as they were at that time. The epics differ in their solution to life's central problem. If *dharma* is observed adequately, it brings order in life, but if it is not followed right it can bring destruction.

The next question we must address is that of heaven. Is it the goal of life? The *Bhagvadagita* does not cast heaven as the permanent abode of the soul in the Hindu system of beliefs. If there is strong attachment to going to heaven, then rebirths, suffering, and the wish to perform meritorious action in order to achieve heaven are all right. One goes to heaven to experience the results of one's meritorious actions. When the *punya*—the merit of righteous action—is used up, one has to return to earth and thus the cycle of rebirth continues. A desire for heaven is not desirable if one does not want to be reborn, although the *Bhagvadagita* says that the desire for heaven is better than other selfish wishes. Thus, the cycle proceeds like this: if one wants to go to heaven, one performs righteous deeds. After the stay in heaven one returns to earth, and takes human form when he is reborn. Eventually, through further righteous deeds, he can attain *moksha*, or liberation from the cycle of rebirth. Thus, Magahi tradition, like other Hindu traditions, produces a mythology that stresses death is divine. Without destruction, there would be no recreation of the universe. It is therefore as divine as creation and sustenance.

My naanii believed in reincarnation. She would tell me many stories that she knew and believed in. Naanii had a very nice attendant named Urmila who was very devoted to her. She was young and affectionate, and naanii spent hours with her. As I have said earlier, naanii was an active and busy housewife. She cooked many delicacies and was usually in the kitchen for long hours. This maidservant was with her in the kitchen. She was naani's companion, and in constantly attending to naanii, Urmila became like a family member. Her husband was also employed with us, and helped naanaa.

Urmila had a very pretty daughter, Sita, who was being raised in naanii's household. Sita was about 10 years old, and everybody loved her. She gave joy to everyone in the house. From the day Sita was born, Urmila, like all mothers, had begun to think of Sita's wedding and had begun to collect as her dowry whatever she could afford. Urmila was hoping that in three to four years Sita would marry and go to her husband's house. Naanii had promised her to help her as much as she could.

Days in naanii's house passed by smoothly. One day it was dusk, not quite dark. The sun was red and round in the sky; we children were playing in the verandah near the kitchen garden. We were playing hide and seek—*luka-chhipi*—trying to hide ourselves in dark corners of the house. We heard Sita screaming. We all assembled there. Urmila and naanii all came. A poisonous snake had bitten Sita. The snake had disappeared in the darkness. But people knew for sure: it was snakebite. Sita was not taken to a hospital. No doctor was called. A famous exorcist came and tried exorcizing for long hours. Saints were called upon to utter *mantras* trying to remove poison from Sita's body. Nothing worked, and by the morning Sita had died; her body was pale and black. Urmila was torn apart, naanii was also very grief-stricken. Sita was gone forever.

It is said time is the biggest healer. A couple of years passed. Urmila got pregnant again. She began thinking that Sita might come back if she was a baby girl. Lo and behold! Urmila delivered a baby girl. Everyone became very happy. Urmila forgot her grief for Sita and started raising the little baby girl. My naanii also was overjoyed. She had faith in reincarnation. She knew Sita has come back in the form of a baby girl.

Naanii related another, very similar story to me. Naanii's sister had a daughter. She was about 10 years old. She got involved in an accident and died. Naanii's sister was severely grief-stricken. The little girl was her only child. After some time, naanii's sister got pregnant. At the time of her delivery, naanii's sister had a dream. In her dream her dead daughter came and said, 'Amma, I am coming back to you. Your dead daughter will come back to you.' My naanii also dreamt a very similar dream at the same time. The delivery took place and naanii's sister gave birth to a baby girl. The family was overjoyed. They welcomed the newly born baby girl with enthusiasm. Their grief had disappeared. They were not disillusioned. They had full faith in reincarnation. They started collecting a dowry for the wedding of the newly born daughter.

Magahi Ballads, Folk Tales, Proverbs and Riddles

Ballads

Ballads were present in ancient Indian literature. The Vedas mention ballads and their significance. The Puranas, which is like an encyclopedia of Hindu mythology, talk about stories of gods in ballad forms. These are tellers of epic stories from the *Ramayana* and from the *Mahabharata*. The bard will intersperse his recitation—which may be performed for several hours days and nights. In the Puranas lots of ballads are mentioned. The *Ramayana* and the *Mahabharata* have composed a lot of ballads. According to this many ballads must be popular but the great composers of epics gave importance to the ballads that were related to Rama's and Krishna's stories. The famous scholar M. Winternitz in his book *History of Indian Literature* (1973) mentions that in ancient India history of ballads were found. For religious or festive occasions religious or heroic ballads were sung with devotion. In fact, popular tales are the basis in the creations of epics like *Ramayana* and *Mahabharata*. Apart from the main story these epics contain a number of legends and episodes that have their basis of popular tales. Many scholars believe that tales of king Nala and the character Karna in the *Mahabharata* are available in various modified forms even today. Stories about many characters in *Mahabharata* and *Ramayana* as also other divine figures like Shiva and Parvati are available in varied forms in many languages and also in Magahi. The folk tale about Shiva and Parvati included in this book is a very good example of that. Another such example is the story about goddesses Saraswati and Lakshmi, which is included in this book.

The Puranas stories later became popular oral tales that

gave rise to various legends in adapted forms. Such popular tales found their greatest expression in the Jataka stories in Buddhist literature. The feature of a main story giving rise to related episodes has evinced in the subsequent famous collections like the *Kathasaritasagara* and *Panchtantra*.

In Pali and Prakrit literature, in the Jataka books there are many ballads that relate the popular stories of Lord Buddha. In the Prakrit period *Gathasaptashati* was the famous collection that had seven hundred beautiful ballads.

From time to time many foreign travelers came to India and have written travelogues. The Chinese traveler Fa-hsien and Hsuan Tsang were famous for their writings. Fa-hsien came at the time of Gupta dynasty. According to him at this time dance, music, songs and ballads were very popular. He has described very vividly about the grandeur of Buddha's reign. Hsuan Tsang came at the time of Harshvardhan's reign. Ballads were very popular in India because of its oral tradition. The listeners of the ballads were mostly upper class elites. Mostly they were kings, ministers, commanders and others. But the singers of the ballads were of lower class and status. Even today this tradition is going on. The composers of the Magahi ballads are not found or known. These ballads change from mouth to mouth. Different singers present different versions of the same ballad. Both vocal and instrumental music are associated with the ballads.

The story of Rama and Sita was taken various shapes in different parts of Bihar. In Munger and Bhagalpur area the folk story of Sita when she was exiled by Rama based on a suspicion that she might be unchaste because of her stay in Lanka is sung very popularly. Sita tried to prove her chastity by entering a blaze of fire. She came out of the fire unhurt. There was another water spring where Sita bathed and by the heat of her body the water became hot. This is the story of 'Sita Kund'.

There is also a story of King Dasharatha. He was unhappy because he did not have offspring. He was blessed by the saint Rishya Sringa and had offspring. This folk story became prevalent. About 40 kilometers away from Munger there is a peak called Sringirikh where Rishya Sringa lived. Thousands of villagers assemble here. There is a spring here. The story is that whoever goes into it whether a child or grown-up, short or tall find the water waist deep. Bathing in this water brings a child to the childless. These stories of ballads were sung by local bards (Chaudhary 1976).

Another story of a local hero Lorik is also very famous. Lorik was born in Dabaur in Gaya district. Lots of ballads are there which are known as 'Lorikayana'. The whole story of Lorik and Chanaini has been put in ballad form by different bards. This ballad is sung not only in Magadh but also in entire north India in all auspicious occasions by Ahirs (milkmen) with great devotion and love. In the entire ballad Lorik, the hero's courage and his magnificent character is described in a song form. It starts with goddess Durga's prayer.

The famous ballad Alha's hero is 'Alha-Udal'. This also starts with a prayer of Rama, Hanuman, Sun and the Ganga. The instrument is a drum. This is a very popular ballad in Magahi areas. People believe that it brings rain if it is sung. It generates heroism and vitality. It mentions many rulers and kings. The important ones are Prithviraj Chauhan, Jayachand and others. Even when it is a Bundel ballad (Bundelkhand is in Madhya Pradesh), it is very popular with Magahi people.

Kumar Vaijee is another heroic ballad but in this the historical aspect is missing. A battle takes place on the occasion of a marriage. The brother and father of Kumar Vaijee are arrested along with other members of the marriage party. At the end, because of his courage Kumar Vaijee comes out as a winner and returns with all the family members, defeating all evil forces. He is dedicated to his wife and protects her from enemies. This is his only goal. It is different from Lorikayan. Lorik's story has a love theme.

Another famous ballad is 'Resma'. This is associated with Doshadh (low) caste people. The hero of this ballad is Chuharmal. He was a great devotee of the goddess Durgaa.

The goddess helped him defeat a powerful landlord Ajabi Singh. It is a love theme ballad.

'Raja Nala' is also quite a renowned ballad. In this fate becomes dominant element. Nala becomes poor but in the end he recovers his wealth and fortune.

'Raja Gopichand' is related to the Nath cult. The king sacrifices royal pleasures and leads a life of a saint (*yogi*). It is a sad ballad. King Gopichand belonged to the Pal dynasty of Bengal.

'Naika Banjara' is a love ballad and associated with oil merchants (*teli*). Sobha and Josomati are the main characters of this ballad. Josomati, the wife of Sobha is driven out of her house when he goes to Morang in the valley of the Himalaya on business. She is driven out on the false charge of adultery. The wife is very devoted to her husband Sobha. She delivers a child. The pang of separation is well depicted in the ballad.

'Bihula' is a ballad famous for the chastity of women. She lengthens her husband's life because of her strong chastity. Bihula is worshipped like a goddess on Nagpanchami day, fifth day of *Savan*.

'Sorthi' is the heroine and Brijabhar is the hero of this ballad. Sorthi, the incarnation of a goddess possesses extraordinary beauty and power. Brijabhar faces lot of difficulties to obtain Sorthi. Even when he is a rich king and becomes mendicant, he underwent a lot of trouble. This ballad is related to Nath cult.

'Baha Bakhtaur' destroyed evil powers like Raja Dalal Singh, Manasa, Hirni and Birni. He is worshipped before starting any sacred work. All Ahirs offer prayer to him. A special kind of drum called *Mandara* is used when this ballad is sung.

Culturally, these ballads were superior to the written literature in many ways. These ballads have rhythm and a very nice musical form. They are narratives and described in such a way that it touches the heart of the village folks. Birds and animals are personified. They talk and add a lot of human touches.

MAGAHI FOLK TALES

If we want to study the culture of India we have to understand the folk tradition, which is oral tradition, and automatically we think of folk tales. Magadh people's life is full of rural episodes. They begin to hear beautiful stories from their grandparents as they are growing up. They attain maturity by listening to these folk tales. By the time they are adults they have a good number of these folk tales into their system. Women start telling suggestive stories on auspicious occasions. This is how the oral tradition of Magahi folktales is adequately maintained. These tales are not merely imaginative but they provide happiness and pleasure at good time and on sad occasions they offer moral strength, peace and patience. Magahi people attain strength and guidance from their ancestors from this form of oral tradition.

India is a country of tales. The Vedas are the most ancient Holy Scriptures in the entire world. In Sanskrit, Pali, Prakrit and Apabhransh literatures the art of tale blossoms and reaches its peak. Magahi literature begins and blossoms from these ancient sources.

There are folk tales of animals also in Magahi, which are very popular. The stories in *Panchtantra* and *Hitopadesha* are collections of excellence. *Panchtantra* is blessed with wonderful tales; it is a gift not only for Indian literature but also for the worldwide literature. They were translated in many languages of the world such as in Arabic, Persian, and Latin and in English. In these stories the narrators are animals and birds. They are moral inducing tales. The *Hitopadesha* stories are also moral stories like *Panchtantra* stories. Magahi people are much influenced by them.

The impact of supernatural beings is also there in Magahi tales. Nothing strikes the child's mind more deeply than the supernatural being. They are flying to the earth and coming to save the princess in agony. When crops fail god 'Indra' is worshipped and it results in heavy rain and thus the crops are saved. The supernatural power is magical. The magical powers of the necklace one wears may have the power to fly. The fairies that are described in Magahi folk tales are very beautiful; they come down to the earth, take a human form. The prince happens to have a glimpse of the fairy in his garden or in his pool; wants to have her and the fairy tale develops.

These tales are very familiar to me as I grew up listening to them from my naanii (grandmother). I am reminded of my childhood and adulthood. Here are some that I will like to share with the readers. Some also appear in Aryani's book (Aryani 1976).

1. There was a king who had four sons. One day he told his sons, 'I have dreamt a dream. There is a country of five fairies. That place has a silver platform. It has a gold tree. The branches of this gold tree are of diamonds. All the leaves have bunches of pearls. Whoever wins this country of diamonds and fairies will obtain my entire throne and he will get married to the fairies.' Three of the king's sons were great friends and got along very well. They had enmity with the youngest one. That is why they pushed him into a well and three of them went on horses to fulfill their father's wish. Fortunately, the youngest son arrives at the fairyland from the route of the well. Other three sons were unsuccessful. At last when the youngest son reaches his father's palace with great difficulty along with the fairies, the three brothers become very envious of him and they make him face a lot of difficult obstacles. But the youngest brother comes out as a winner. The king, the father very happily marries him with the fairies and gives him his throne. The king's dream gets fulfilled.
2. This story is regarding the 'Teej' festival, Goddess Parvati's worship is very significant here. Parvati's mother tried her best to find a husband for her but could not succeed. All her attempts failed. One day Parvati went to a jungle with her friends. Lord Shiva was practicing *tapasyaa* (religious austerities) in the same jungle. When Parvati saw him she

fell in love with him. She began to observe 'Teej' festival in order to attain Lord Shiva. Lord Shiva was very pleased with her and married her. The festival of 'Teej' is observed by all Magahi married women (*suhagin*) for the welfare and long life of their husbands. The festival of 'Teej' falls in the third day of lunar fortnight in the month of *Savan* (July and August).

3. Here is another story that is about the festival of 'Jitia'. It is also a very important *vrata* (observance). There were two sisters named Chilho and Siyaro. Chilho had seven sons. She used to observe 'Jitia' festival every year and do fasting for the entire day and night. Siyaro was barren and had no children. She was also very greedy and would break her fasting to eat good food. Siyaro got very envious of her sister Chilho's seven sons and got them killed. But because of Chilho's intense faith and devotion for the festival of 'Jitia' all her dead children became alive. This *vrata* is also a very important one for Magahi mothers. It lengthened the lives of their children. It is a fast and is kept by mothers for their children so that they attain long life. It falls in *Bhado* (August and September).
4. *The 'Vrata' ChhaTh*: A barren woman promised a vow to worship Sun god and observe 'ChhaTh' festival every year. She was blessed with a son. But after his birth she forgot to keep her vow. The boy even got married. He was returning home with his newly married wife, but he died on his way. When the mother ChhaTh heard the newly married girl cry, she said, 'Your mother-in-law forgot her promise and hence your husband died. If you promise to worship me your husband would become alive'. She kept her promise. The festival of ChhaTh falls in the month of *Kartik* (October and November). It is celebrated to worship *Surya-dev* (Sun god).
5. *The Saint*: Once upon a time there was a hermit who lived in a little hut in a village of Magadh. He would go to beg his bread everyday. Whatever he got he would eat in the noon and also save some for his evening meal. And out of

that food he would give a portion to any visitor who came to his hut. There lived an old woman in the same village. She had an only son who lived in the city to earn money. One day the saint went to the old lady to beg. She didn't give alms to him because she didn't like him. She gave the saint some bread mixed with poison. The lady wanted to get rid of the saint. The saint had no knowledge of the poisoned bread. He kept the bread for visitors. Very soon the old woman's son came to his hut. The son was hungry and thirsty. The saint gave him the poisoned bread and water. The old woman's son died after eating the bread. The old lady found out that her son had eaten the bread she gave to the saint. She wept bitterly and realized the sin she had committed.

6. *The Beggar*: There was a beggar who used to go out and beg everyday. He was very religious and everyday he would offer a little amount of food to Lord Shiva at his shrine. Goddess Parvati, Lord Shiva's wife was very overwhelmed at this. She said to Lord Shiva, 'Let us help this beggar'. Lord Shiva said, 'O.K. let us give him some gold'. They both came and dropped a lump of gold on the street where the beggar used to pass by. The beggar as he was going to his daily round remembered a blind man who happened to walk on the same street. Trying to imitate the blind man, the beggar closed his eyes and started walking on the street. Naturally he missed the gold. Soon a merchant came and saw the gold, he quickly picked it up. Lord Shiva said to Parvati, 'See Parvati, the beggar was not destined to be a rich man even when god gave him. Fate didn't let him be rich.' A lot of Magahi folk tales are given in the second section of this book.

Magahi Riddles and Proverbs

The riddles and proverbs have been a subject of interest as forms of folklore to folklorists. Magahi has very interesting collections of riddles and proverbs. When actually they originated, it is very difficult to say. The use of riddles on ceremonial occasions is described in *Rig Veda*. The tradition of riddles and religion continued well in the eleventh century. The use of riddles was found in ancient literature. In the epics, the *Mahabharata* and *Ramayana* one finds hundreds of riddle verses. Ancient poets were expected to do the art of riddling. Ban Bhatt's *Kadambari*, a seventh-century (*c.* AD 600–650) Sanskrit romance riddling is composed with a lot of maturity and excellence. The best-known Hindi riddle collections were by Amir Khusrau (1255–1306).

Riddling was very common in Magahi also and it continues to be popular among the people of all ages and castes. They could also be of different classes. Who has composed them is not very clear to anyone. In Magahi folk literature, riddles and proverbs are given much importance.

The primary function of riddling in villages also in cities of this region is competition and entertainment. After the evening meal, riddling may begin. All the members of the family and their guests may participate. Usually a person will pose a riddle to someone and he is expected to solve it. It also can take place outside of home. In winter, a group of people would sit around a fire, adults smoking *bidis* or *hookahs* and enjoying riddling. Generally men participate in it. If it takes place outside where visitors present themselves, it provides a good opportunity for new riddles from the community. Here are some very popular Magahi riddles in translation:

1. *kariyaa bilaai ke hariar puunch.* (Translation: A black cat has a green tail.)
   This riddle stands for a palm tree that has green leaves on a dark trunk.
2. *laRkaa he pet meN, daaRhii uRe havaa meN.* (Translation: The child in the womb has his beard blowing in the wind.) This stands for corn on the cob with its kernel still intact. The kernels are like children in the covered womb with the corn silk blowing in the wind.

3. *ek ghaRaa me du rung paanii.* (Translation: There is a pitcher in which there is water of two colors, white and yellow.)
   In the egg, there is egg white and egg yolk.
4. *haraa DanTii laal kamaan tobaa tobaa kare Kamaan.* (Translation: On a green stem there is a red bow. Even the brave [after tasting it] vows to sin no more.)
   The answer of this riddle is red pepper.
5. *laal chhaRii, maidaan gaRii.* (Translation: There is a red stick, which is grounded in the field.) The answer is a sweet potato. It is of red color and grows in the ground.

Magahi proverbs also are very interesting. They are found in abundance. It makes the literature colorful and influences the entire culture of oral tradition. The proverbs provide the lifestyle of the villagers. These unlettered folks are rich in wisdom. Sometimes Magahi proverbs are episodic like Magahi folk tales. A famous proverb reads as follows: When a Koirin's (low caste) daughter went to the king's house she began to call an eggplant (*baiNgan*) *TaiNgan* (nonsense rhyme).

The story is that there was a daughter of *koirin* (vegetable vendor) who was very beautiful. The king got enchanted by her beauty and married her and took her to his palace. She had become very conceited by her present position. One day as she was walking around her balcony she heard her mother the *koirin*, 'Here is *baiNgan* (eggplants)'. *Koirin's* daughter heard this and murmured, 'Oh, here goes *baiNgan TaiNgan* again'.

Proverbs

1. *koirin ke betii raajaa ghar gel to baiNgan ke TaiNgan kahlak.* (Translation: When Koirin [lower caste] girl happens to be married in a royal family tries to give *baiNgan* [eggplant] an insulting name *TaiNgan*, which means nothing.)
2. *kahaaN raajaa bhoj aaur kahaaN bhojwaa telii.* (Translation:

How is a lowly oil seller comparable to a king just because they share the same name *bhoj*.)

3. *adhjal gagrii chhalkat jaae*. (Translation: A half-filled pitcher spills a lot.) A comparable saying in English is: An empty vessel makes much noise.
4. *kaa barkhaa jab kinkhii sukhaane*. (Translation: What use is rain after the crop is already dried and lost.)
5. *teen kanaujia terah chuulhaa*. (Translation: Only three Kannauj dwellers but they have thirteen separate kitchens). This comments on the fact that the Brahmins of the place Kannauj are such sticklers that they can't get along.
6. *chaubejii gelan chhabbe hove, duube ho ke ailan*. (Translation: 'Chaube' wanted to proceed to become 'Chhabbe' but ended up coming back as a 'Dube'.)
   It comments on people getting diminished while trying to over-achieve Chaube is the epithet for a person who has mastered the four Vedas. Dube is one who has mastered only two. Chabbe would refer to someone who has mastered six Vedas, but there are only four Vedas and not six.

These riddles and proverbs would fill us with jubilance and joy as we indulged in them. We would start saying these riddles and proverbs when we gathered in fairs and festivals, weddings and religious ceremonies. It provided sense of competition and a lot of entertainment. All our family members, friends and relatives will look forward to participating in them. One person would pose a riddle to someone of any age younger or older and ask him or her to solve. Family members who knew the answer would refrain themselves to give it. These riddles will provide excitement. For younger children, they were like games trying to solve puzzles. Usually there is some pleasurable surprise in hearing the answer. Occasionally there is some dispute about the aptness of the answer and the 'riddler' may even be asked to prove that the answer is correct. If the guesser answers the riddle correctly, then there may be exclamations of praise for him by the entire group. Most of the time there is no order in choosing who will pose the riddle. Anyone can pose a riddle. Sometimes a prize is offered for the successful solution and a punishment is threatened for those who fail to solve the riddle. This kind of riddling offered a lot of fun and we would look forward to this kind of Magahi gatherings and get-togethers.

Conclusion

Magahi folklore is rich in tradition. Its ancient folk music, cultural diversity and strong heritage have made it extremely colorful and enchanting. Traditional folk music when passed on by ear and performed by memory rather than written literature makes it very rich. Folk music, folk art, folk instruments are all varied and diverse. The decorative paintings in rural homes have both aesthetic and ritualistic cultural effect. Although the motifs of such painting might vary from one region to another, the basic art reflects the same structurally. The snake and sparrow motif is predominant in one area while the animal, tree and flower motifs seem to dominate in the other direction. The ritualistic *rangoli*, the *mehendi* decorations on bride's hands for festive occasions are some of the best examples of the Magahi folklore culture.

Magadh, actually the entire India for that matter occupies a special place in the history of world folklore. The marvelous India tale has contributed in shaping the growth of folkloristics. Lots of eminent writers, for instance, Max Müller's works on Indian myth and Theoder Benfrey's translation of the famous *Panchtantra* gave the Indian origin of fairy tales. India also possessed the oldest written oral tradition in the world. The *Rig Veda*, the *Ramayana* and *Mahabharata*, the Puranas and Upanishads, *Hitopadesha*, *Kathaasaṛita Saagara*, Jataka and many others are the best examples. Also because of the multiplicity of languages the culture has gotten enriched. History tells us how these cultural differences made it interesting and how it influenced the folk language.

Alexander (326 BC) opened the gateway to Western influences. His invasion was the result of the establishment of the Indian empires under great kings like Chandragupta Maurya and Ashoka. Ashoka's empire spread Buddhist thought also which established itself as the world's greatest religion. Then came the prosperous and great kings like Guptas making the age very rich. Then came the Turks, Mughals, the Dutch, Portuguese, French and the British. A lot of changes took place. Different empires and kingdoms came. They influenced India culturally. The culture became richer and richer because of these diverse heritage.

Not much was done to retain the rich oral tradition. Unfortunately, Magahi folklore also was declining rapidly. The missionaries tried to do some work in this direction. Despite their efforts to save the rich folklore and its oral tradition it was disappearing fast. No country in the eastern civilization offers such an excellent variety of folklore as does India, specially Magadh. It had added vigour and vitality age after age in Magadh areas. While studies on Indian caste system, social structure, kinship, village organization, etc., received the attention of both Western and Indian scholars, oral traditions unfortunately were being neglected. Scholars seemed to have failed to understand that a systematic study of oral traditions would have contributed immensely to retain the rich Magadh culture.

In recent years much after the country gained freedom, the reconstruction of past history has become the concern of people. The intelligentsia now makes such reconstructions. India has a glorious past, so has Magadh. Of course, the present has to be beautiful also. This beauty lies in language, food, dress, oral tradition, literature and many aspects of life. It was after the mid-1950s when folklore began to be studied consistently. The strength of Indian culture cannot be measured only by non-Indian standards. It has to be measured or judged by its own standards. Folklore study began with the arrival of the British. Magahi also started its folklore study at that time. The works of the missionaries and civil servants of course explored folklore not only in India but of different regional linguistic areas also. The more Indian scholars became aware of their cultural roots the more they wanted to be free both culturally and politically. Magadh, and for that matter, entire India suddenly became aware of its negligence. Native speakers inspired by the nationalistic movements, valued their oral traditions and began collecting and studying them. They started contributing their ideas not only in their national language but also in their national epics, food, dress, etc. One of the major achievements of free India has been to preserve the cultural diversities and Magadhi folklore has become a field to be studied by researchers and students of folklore. Now it has added prestige to the discipline and will help enhance the growth of Magadh and its folklore. The cultural milieu of Magadh has been recognized and it is in the right direction of progress. Soon it will be taught in colleges and universities for higher degrees. The scientific approach to oral tradition, which our modern scholars are committed to, has not been accomplished fully. Magadh folklore due to the reasons of its ancient past has great potential for its culture. The manner in which Magadhi folklore studies have taken up in the past few years indicates promise and a bright future.

Some Favorite Recipes from the Magahi Cuisine

The recipes I include here come from my childhood. Some of my fondest early memories are of my grandmother cooking in an elaborate kitchen. She sat in front of a clay *chulhaa*, or stove, on a low wooden stool with a colorful cushion.

An Indian morning begins very early. It starts out at five or six o'clock, winter or summer. Naanaa and naanii started out by bathing in warm water that had been heated by servants who had risen even earlier. They then did their morning *puja* (prayers and worship) and got ready to eat. Naanii wanted us to get ready before we ate breakfast. Even her cook had to bathe before entering the kitchen.

Naanaa and naanii never drank tea. When my parents came to stay with naanii and naanaa, they were offered milky tea in the morning. We children never had tea. Of course, nowadays in the US, we make a big fuss over tea. I put a large teapot on a silver tray with tea cozy to keep the tea hot. I place cups and a silver sugar bowl and creamer on the tray, and then we make our tea in a leisurely manner. It takes us an hour to finish drinking.

We used the *chakki*—the grinding stone—very efficiently to grind fresh bulk spices, grains, and lentils. We stored what we had ground in a storeroom next to the kitchen. There was another, smaller *chakki* with a pestle that we could use to make wet, ground *masala* (spices) called *silaut* and *lorha*.

All the kitchen activities started in the morning. The maidservants took charge of grinding *masalas*, while the servants would be busy doing other kitchen things. There was a cook who did the actual cooking. Everyone in the kitchen would be busy listening to naanii's delicious recipes and instructions.

In another corner of the kitchen was a large, wooden shelf where we stored washed, glittering pots and pans. There, shiny *thaalis* and *katoris*—metal plates and bowls—shone on the shelf. We stored the spices on another shelf. Lots of jars with different spices of six different colors were stacked in a very organized way.

The most striking variation we find in Magahi cooking, and in most Indian cooking, for that matter, is the list of spices, fresh or dried, whole or ground, that accompanies each recipe. Some are familiar—cinnamon, clove, ginger, nutmeg, cumin, cardamom, coriander, and turmeric. Others are not found anywhere except in specialty shops, such as asafoetida, black cardamom, and fenugreek.

Naanii grew fresh herbs in her vegetable garden. Fresh leaves of cilantro, mint, garlic greens, scallions, leek, fenugreek, and red chilies arrived in the house daily to comprise part of the traditional Magahi palette of seasonings.

On the spice shelf in almost every Magahi kitchen, and in kitchens across Bihar, are also jars of turmeric, or *haldi*. People used to grind turmeric and make fresh, wet *masala* to cook vegetables and dal. One may wonder why turmeric is so prevalent in the cuisine of the region. Believe it or not, dishes with *haldi* are very tasty and healthy—indeed, bestselling author Dr. Nicholas Perricone commends turmeric as the 'antioxidant king' in his book *The Perricone Promise*. Lots of north Indian pickles, chutneys, curries, and gravies require *haldi*. Without *haldi*, northern Indian food can be very bland.

Small, puffed puris fried in pure ghee, delicious vegetables, *dahi* (curd or yogurt), *halwa* and seasonal fresh fruit were served for breakfast. Naanii made her own fresh *dahi* everyday, and always served it with breakfast, and frequently with other meals, as well.

For lunch, the menu often read as follows: basmati rice, plain rice (*bhaat*), or sometimes rice fried with almonds and saffron and raisins; dal seasoned with pure ghee and dry spices; vegetable *bhujia* with freshly ground turmeric and other spices, and homemade *dahi*. For dessert, coconut sweets in various forms were naanii's favorite delicacy, while shredded coconut cooked in milk and sugar was her most popular dessert.

A typical dinner consisted of *roti* (unleavened bread), dal, and tasty vegetables of different varieties, sweets, and Indian puddings.

Magahi meals are served all at once, not course by course, although dessert was always served at the end. Food was served in a *thaali*, or on a silver plate arranged and set with several small metal bowls containing the dal, assorted vegetables, salad, *raita* (vegetables, cucumbers, and yogurt), pickles, and chutney. These meals are really quite a beautiful sight. Great care is taken in serving the food, and cleanliness is strictly observed, both for hygienic and religious reasons.

Many of my family's recipes are vegetarian, as both of my parents were vegetarians, although a lot of Magahi people eat meat. The traditional Indian style of eating is with one's fingers, although this is done fastidiously. Hands are washed before and after meals, and after eating, one is expected to wash one's mouth, also.

As I have noted earlier, my naanii loved to cook vegetables, cereals, and protein-generating food. Each of these groups had extra importance of their own when meat, fish, poultry and eggs were missing from the cuisine. Magahi cuisine has limitless variety of food, and I am introducing recipes which I am sure people in the west would love to cook. They will be tasty, and with a little careful variation, can be low in calories, also.

I. VEGETABLES

Aloo Bhujia with Lahsun Patta
(picy Sautéed Potato with Garlic Greens)

1 lb small potatoes cut in halves
2 oz mustard or olive oil
1 tsp turmeric powder
1 tsp chili powder

½ tsp cumin seed
½ tsp fenugreek seed
2–4 whole dry red peppers
½ bag of chopped garlic greens (frozen)
Masala paste:
  1 tsp ground turmeric powder
  1 tsp garlic powder
  ½ tsp chili powder
  Salt to taste
  1 tsp water, mixed well with the powdered spices

Wash the potatoes and cut them in halves or fourths. Heat the oil and add the cumin seed, fenugreek seeds, and whole peppers. When they brown, add the potatoes. When the potatoes are almost cooked, add thawed chopped garlic greens. After five minutes, add *masala* paste. Cook for five more minutes, stirring well. Serve with rice, dal, or *puris* and *rotis*.

Bhujia can be made without garlic greens. *Aloo bhujia* can also be made with *methi* (fenugreek greens) or spinach.

Potato *bhujia* with cubed eggplant (*baigan*) tastes equally good. The method is the same as above; simply add the cubed eggplant when you add the potatoes. Gobhi (cauliflower) *Bhujia* also can be made the same way. The cauliflower should be cut in medium-sized florets.

Spinach or Mustard Saag (Greens)

1 bag of chopped *palak* (spinach greens), either frozen or fresh
2 tsp of olive oil or mustard oil
1 tsp cumin seeds
1 tsp fenugreek seeds
4 dry red peppers

Heat oil in a wok or skillet, and add seasonings until it starts crackling. After the seasonings brown, add the thawed greens and cook until tender. Add salt to taste.

Aloo Bharta (Mashed Potatoes with Condiments)

4 medium-sized potatoes
1 large onion, chopped
2 dry red roasted peppers (optional)
1 tsp mustard oil

Peel the potatoes and cut them into quarters. Boil them. Mash them smoothly. Mix the chopped onions, and roasted chopped pepper in the mashed potatoes. Mix in the mustard oil, and add salt to taste.

Baigan Bharta (Mashed Eggplant)

Cut one large eggplant into two pieces. Grill or broil it in the oven. Test it with a knife. When it's cooked, leave the skin on and mash it. Add the ingredients as described above.

Tamatar Bharta (Roasted, Mashed Tomato)

Roast or broil two large tomatoes in the oven. Peel and mash them. Mix chopped onion, chopped fresh garlic (2 cloves), pepper, mustard oil and salt. Add chopped fresh coriander leaves.

Aloo Tarkari (Potato Curry)

4 large potatoes
2 medium onions
1 inch fresh ginger, grated
1 tsp cumin seed
2 bay leaves
2 tomatoes
½ cup plain yogurt
¼ cup olive oil
1 tsp *garam masala* (available in Indian stores, or else blend ground cardamom, cloves, cinnamon, and cumin)
½ tsp chili powder

Peel potatoes and cut them into quarters. Boil them. Heat oil and add cumin seed; brown the cumin seed and add round onion rings into the oil. Add grated ginger. Mix the boiled potatoes in. Cook for five minutes, and then add the halved tomatoes and spices. Add yogurt and cook for five minutes. Sprinkle with chopped coriander leaves, and serve with rice.

Ghant (Mixed Vegetables)

1 large eggplant, cubed
1 package green beans or lima beans, frozen
1 package chopped spinach, frozen
1 tsp cumin seed
½ tsp fenugreek seed
1 tsp aniseed
2-3 red peppers
½ cup mustard oil
Masala paste

Heat oil and add seasonings until they brown. Add cubed eggplant and let it brown. Add thawed beans and chopped spinach. Mix the vegetables with *masala* paste. Cook it until the vegetables are tender, and the water is absorbed.

II. SALADS AND CHUTNEYS

Cucumber Raita

1 cucumber
1 cup plain yogurt
½ tsp roasted ground cumin
chopped mint leaves
1 tsp sugar
Salt to taste

Wash the cucumber well. Shred it into coarse strips with a

grater; it is not necessary to peel the cucumber. You can also chop the cucumber if you prefer. Squeeze the grated cucumber and remove all the water. Place the yogurt in a bowl and mix it thoroughly with a fork. Mix cumin powder, salt, and sugar in the yogurt. Mix cucumber well. Garnish it with cumin powder, red pepper powder, and mint leaves.

Potato Raita

You can make this dish with the same method. Boil the potatoes and peel them. Cut them into small cubes. Add them into the yogurt with the above spices.

Cucumber, Tomato, and Onion Salad with Moong Beans

1 cucumber, peeled and chopped
1 tomato, cut into small pieces
½ red onion, chopped
Coriander leaves, chopped
1 green pepper, chopped
2 tsp moong beans, sprouted
1 tsp lemon juice
1 tsp balsamic vinegar
1 tsp sugar
salt to taste

Mix all the ingredients in a bowl. Add lemon juice, vinegar, salt, and sugar. Garnish it with chopped coriander leaves.

Fresh Coriander Chutney

1 cup chopped coriander leaves
1 green pepper, cut
¼ cup of shredded coconut, fresh or dry
½ large onion, chopped
½ tsp salt
1 tsp lemon juice

Blend together the ingredients, adding lemon juice and water gradually, until you arrive at a smooth paste. Serve the chutney in a small bowl with meals or snacks.

Fresh Mint Chutney

This chutney can be made as described above if you simply substitute 1 cup chopped mint leaves for the coriander leaves.

Sweet Tomato Chutney

3–4 medium tomatoes
1 inch fresh, grated ginger
1 tsp yellow raisins
3–4 whole, dry red peppers
Fresh, chopped coriander leaves
1 tsp cumin powder
1 tsp curry powder
1 cup sugar
salt to taste

In a saucepan, heat sugar and ¼ cup of water. Let it boil. Add sliced tomatoes and fresh, grated ginger. Add cumin powder, curry powder, and whole red peppers. Add salt and raisins. Cook until smooth and sticky. Add chopped coriander leaves before serving.

III. DALS (LENTIL SOUPS)

There are different kinds of dals in the Magahi cuisine. Dal is eaten with rice or *roti* daily.

Gughni (*Black Curried Chick Peas; also called Kala Chanaa*)

1 cup *kala chanaa* (available in Indian stores)
¼ cup mustard or olive oil
1 large onion sliced

1 tsp garlic powder
1 tsp coriander powder
1 tsp cumin powder
1 inch fresh ginger, grated
½ tsp turmeric powder
Red pepper powder to taste
Salt to taste

Soak *kala chanaa* overnight. Drain the water in the morning. In a saucepan, heat oil. Add sliced onions and sauté. Add grated ginger. Put soaked *kala chanaa* in the saucepan. Cook for ten minutes. Add all the spices and continue sautéing at a medium heat until the *chanaa* and spices are almost cooked. Add 1 cup of water and cook until the water is almost absorbed. Serve with rice or roti.

Rahar Dai

1 cup rahar dal (available in Indian stores)
3 cups of hot water
1 tsp turmeric powder
Salt to taste

Cook dal in water with turmeric powder and salt. When dal is cooked and mixed well, season it with very hot mustard oil. Add cumin seed or *garam masala*, add 3 to 4 hot peppers to the oil, and stir until they brown. Mix them in the dal in a saucepan.

Yellow Split Pea Dal

Can be made as described above.

Red Masoor Lentils

Red masoor lentils are available at Indian or specialty stores. This dal can be made in the same way as described above.

IV. FISH & MEAT

Fish Curry

1 lb catfish cut into 2-inch filets
½ cup mustard powder
2 tsp garlic powder
1 tsp turmeric powder
½ tsp red pepper powder
2 fresh medium tomatoes
½ cup mustard oil
Coriander leaves, chopped
Salt to taste

Make a smooth paste of mustard powder, turmeric, garlic, pepper, and a little water in a bowl. Add salt. Marinate fish pieces in the paste.

Heat mustard oil in a deep skillet. Add marinated fish fillets to the heated oil. Brown them on both sides carefully, and try to keep the fish from breaking. Add 1 cup of water to the skillet to make more gravy. Add halved tomatoes and coriander leaves. The gravy should be thick, not watery.

You can make fish fry in the same way—simply do not add water to make gravy.

Serve with plain rice.

Chicken Curry

1 lb boneless chicken cut into 1-inch pieces
2 large onions, sliced
2 inches of ginger, grated
10 large, fresh garlic cloves, grated
1 tsp turmeric powder
½ tsp red pepper
1 tsp *garam masala* powder
2 medium tomatoes, cubed
Coriander leaves, chopped

¼ cup mustard or olive oil
Salt to taste

In a saucepan, heat oil and sauté onions, ginger, and garlic. Add chicken pieces. Cook covered and at medium heat. Add turmeric and red pepper. After some time, add *garam masala*. Add tomatoes and coriander. Let it simmer until the chicken is cooked. Add water. When the gravy has thickened, serve with rice.

V. RICE DISH

Matar Pulao (*Fried Rice with Peas*)

9 oz basmati rice
3 oz ghee (clarified butter)
1 tsp salt
6 cloves
12 peppercorns
1 tsp cinnamon powder
⅔ pint of water (or twice the quantity of rice)
6 oz shelled peas
2 cardamom seeds
Saffron
Chopped almonds
1 tsp cumin seeds
4 oz thinly sliced onion

Clean, wash, and soak rice for ½ hour in water. Save the water.

Heat the ghee and fry the onions in it. When they are brown, add cardamoms, cloves, and peppercorns. Add peas and continue frying for five minutes. Add rice, salt, and cinnamon for five minutes. Add the water in which the rice was soaked and cook. Add saffron and almonds.

VI. SNACKS

Thekua

The recipe for this cookie-like snack is provided in the Fairs and Festivals chapter.

Nimki

8 oz of wheat flour
½ tsp *kalaunji* or *mangraila* (available at Indian or specialty stores)
¼ cup ghee or olive oil
Salt to taste
Extra ghee for frying

Mix salt and *mangraila* into the flour. Slowly mix the ghee into the flour, as well. Add water to make a soft dough. Knead well.

Make large balls of dough. On a cutting board, roll the dough out until it is ½ inch thick. Cut long, ½ inch wide stips. Deep fry them in ghee until they brown. Serve them with tea or coffee.

Fried ChuRaa (Beaten or Flat Rice fried)

1 cup ghee
½ cup beaten rice (available in Indian sores)
Salt and ground pepper to taste

Heat ghee until it is very hot. Add one teaspoon beaten rice into the hot ghee. Fry it. Take the rice out of the ghee quickly. Strain it with a *jhanjara*, a flat, grooved spatula (available in Indian stores). The beaten rice comes out flaky and crisp. Add salt and pepper. Eat it with sautéed peas or germinated *moong* beans.

Sautéed Matar (Peas)

1 bag frozen peas, thawed
1 onion, chopped
2 tsp ghee
1 inch fresh ginger, grated
1 tsp cumin seed
1 green pepper
Chopped coriander leaves

In a skillet, heat ghee and sauté onions and ginger. Add peas and continue sautéing for 5 minutes. Add coriander leaves and green pepper. Serve it with fried *ChuRaa.*

Moong Sprouts, Sautéed

Soak 1 cup of whole, dry moong beans in water overnight. Drain water, put it in a large bowl, and leave it inside a cool oven overnight. The moong will sprout.

Sauté the germinated moong using the same method as described above for sautéed matar. Serve it very warm—it makes a healthy snack.

VI. DESSERT

Puaa

1 cup of wheat flour
1 cup of brown sugar
Ghee
Milk
Raisins
1 tsp of Aniseed

Make a thick batter with flour, brown sugar, and milk. Add raisins and aniseeds. Heat ghee and put on tablespoon (or more) of batter in the ghee. Let the batter brown, then remove it. One cup of flour will make several round *puaas*. Serve them warm.

Jalebi

1 lb flour
½ oz yeast
1 pinch of saffron
3–4 cardamom, powdered
2 tsp sour yogurt
1 lb sugar
Ghee to fry *jalebi* in

Dissolve the yeast in warm water. Make batter with flour, yeast, and yogurt. Add ground saffron. Leave the batter for an hour or so. Make syrup using sugar and 1 pint of water. Boil it, but do not let it get too thick. Add saffron and cardamom powder. Heat the oil. Pour the batter from a plastic bottle with a narrow nozzle (like a ketchup or mustard squeeze bottle). Make 3–4 rounds of batter in the oil, and let them brown. Take them out of the ghee and leave them in the warm syrup to harden. This is an extremely popular dessert.

Suji Halva (Semolina or Cream of Wheat Halwa)

4 oz cream of wheat
4 oz sugar
A pinch of saffron
4 oz of ghee
⅔ pint of water
1 oz almonds, chopped and peeled
4 cardamoms

Mix sugar and water. Add cardamoms. Simmer until sugar is dissolved. Add saffron.

In a skillet, add ghee and heat it and add cream of wheat. Stir on slow heat until the mixture gets light brown. Add syrup and stir briskly. Mix in almonds. Serve the *halwa* warm.

Suji Kheer

4 oz cream of wheat
4 oz of sugar
Pinch of saffron
2 oz ghee
1 pint of milk
1 oz of almond
Raisins (optional)

In a saucepan, heat ghee and add cream of wheat. Stir it on a low heat. When it gets brown, add milk, sugar, almonds, and saffron. Keep stirring until cream of wheat gets cooked. You may add more milk to make the consistency of the *kheer* thinner. Serve *kheer* warm or cold.

Rice Kheer

1½ oz Basmati rice
1½ pint milk
2 cardamom seeds
2 oz sugar
Saffron (optional)

Wash and soak rice in ¼ pint of water. Boil milk and add rice in it. Add cardamoms. Cook rice ih milk until rice is cooked and milk is thick. Add sugar and cook until it is dissolved. The consistency should be like the cream of wheat *kheer*. Chill and refrigerate. Serve it in small bowls.

Sevai Kheer (Vermicelli)

4 oz fine vermicelli (available in Indian or specialty stores)
2 pints milk
4 oz sugar
1 oz ghee
1 oz almonds

In a saucepan, add ghee and *sevai* until the *sevai* is lightly brown. Add milk and boil it until the *sevai* is cooked and the milk gets thickened. Add sugar, cardamoms, and almonds. Serve warm or cold.

PART II

MAGAHI FOLK TALES

The Seven Swans

There was a king. He was fond of hunting. One day while hunting he got lost in a jungle. He came across a hut and inside the hut he saw an old woman sitting. She was a wizard. The king asked her for help in finding his way back. The old woman said, 'Yes, I will show you the way, but on one condition. If you don't listen to me then you will die of hunger and thirst in this jungle'.

The king asked her what her condition was. She said that the king would have to marry her only daughter. The king had no choice but to marry the old woman's daughter. The king reached his destination with the old woman's daughter, and there they were married.

The king had eight children from his first queen—seven sons and a daughter. The king loved them very much, and thought that their new stepmother might torture them. So he built another palace in a jungle for the children. The children lived in that new palace very happily. The king urged to visit them frequently. The new queen came to know about this. One day when the king went hunting the new queen went to the children's palace. The children came running to her thinking that their father had come. As they came closer to her, the queen by the force of magic transformed them into seven swans and made them fly. Feeling happy and content, she returned to her palace.

The king's daughter was watching all this from her window where she used to sit. The princess felt unable to live in that palace and left right away. She grew very tired walking. She arrived at a larger palace and entered. She saw seven beds in that palace. She lay on one of the beds. Suddenly she saw seven swans fluttering their wings on the window and fall on the beds. They were transformed into handsome princes. The princess and the princes immediately recognized each other and were happy. The brothers asked the sister to leave as soon as possible. The brothers said, 'There are seven giants who reside here. They will be coming here soon. They will be after you. We seven brothers become human beings for a little while, then we become swans again.'

The princess asked her brothers when they would be changed back into human beings permanently. The brothers answered, 'If you go straightly from here, you will find a hut. In that hut there will be an old woman spinning cotton. You ask for spun cotton, and for seven years you spin seven shirts without laughing or speaking to anybody. We will wear those shirts and be transformed into human beings. If you laugh or speak then we won't be transformed into human beings.' After saying this, the seven brothers were transformed into swans, and they flew.

The princess went looking for the hut in that jungle. Finally, after a lot of searching, she found it. She told the old woman everything. The old woman gave her some cotton, which she had spun. Under a tree, the princess quietly started spinning cotton for shirts. She would not smile or talk to anyone.

After a few days the king of that region came to hunt. He asked the princess who she was. But the princess did not answer him. She was very beautiful. The king wanted to marry her and so he brought her to his palace. Their wedding took place with pomp and grandeur. The princess after some time delivered a beautiful son.

The king's mother was a very jealous woman. She asked herself: 'what kind of a princess is this, who is very quiet always and does not speak or laugh or smile?' One day the princess was sleeping, the king's mother entered her room and hid the little baby and smeared blood in the mouth of the princess. She created a lot of noise and told the king that the princess was demoness; she killed her son and ate it. The king seeing blood in her mouth got very enraged. He ordered a flayer to kill her. This day was the last day of the seven years.

Seven shirts were ready now. As soon as the flayer was going to kill the princess, all the seven swans came fluttering and flying. The princess threw the shirts towards the seven swans. Her brothers wore the shirts and were transformed into seven handsome princes. They embraced the sister. The flayer was at his wit's end seeing all this and he called the king. The princess told the king everything. The king was delighted to hear all this. The king's mother was very happy seeing all this and asked for forgiveness. She brought the baby. The king, queen, his mother, and the seven princes were very pleased and lived their lives happily ever after.

The Cock and the Gold Nugget

There was a king. He had many queens. One of the queens had a son who used to be a cock during the day and a man at night. One day the cock went out grazing. He found a gold nugget in the way. He brought it home and kept it. The next day he went out and found another gold nugget. He picked up the nugget and went further. He met a man. The cock asked him to fill his ears with rice and offered him the gold nugget.

A princess saw this and asked her mother to fill the cock's ear with rice and get the gold nugget. She started filling his ear with rice, but could not fill it. She exhausted the king's entire storage of rice and still could not fill the cock's ear. Finally the cock asked her to fill his ear with more handful of rice, and this time the ear got filled. The cock gave her the gold nugget and went ahead.

He ran into a goat shepherd. He sent the shepherd home to his mother with the message that she should empty all the rice containers and storage places of rice. He needed to store all the rice he had in his ear. The mother asked how a mere cock could bring so much rice and grain. The cock arrived and said, 'Empty all the containers, mother. Here is the rice I brought.' He shook his ear and the entire palace and courtyard were filled with rice. The distant relatives and neighborhood people assembled and could not believe their eyes when they saw so much rice. They started hitting their own children with malice and said, 'You are human beings and don't do anything and here is a mere cock who brings so much rice!'

The next day the cock with his first gold nugget went another direction. He came to the kingdom of another king. The king's daughter said, 'Oh my, a cock is selling gold nuggets for a handful of rice!' So the entire stock of rice was poured into the cock's ear, but the ear would not fill and everyone was puzzled. The cock said, 'One more handful of rice in my ear, please', and the ear filled. The cock gave her the gold nugget and went ahead.

He found another cow shepherd and sent to his mother the same message, 'Empty all the storage places of rice.' He shook his ear and filled the place with rice. The relatives and neighbors got envious and reacted the same way. 'A mere cock can do it and you human children can't!'

The cock proceeded to another direction. He found a scorpion and the scorpion said to him, 'Oh cock, dear, where are you going?' The cock answered that he was going to his in-law's house. The friendly scorpion accompanied him and sat in his ear. Then the cock ran into a serpent. The serpent also sat in the cock's ear. After this a stick sat in his ear. Later a tiger requested the cock take him along. In the same way, fire also got into his ear.

The cock arrived at the king's palace and expressed that he wanted to marry his daughter, the princess. The princess said to him, 'How can you marry me—you are a mere cock!' Hearing this, the cock released all the ferocious beings from his ear. The tiger started eating everybody, the scorpion began to bite, and the fire began to burn. There was an old lady who was saved, and she fell on the feet of the cock and said to him that he could marry the princess if he saved everyone. The cock did, and accordingly married the princess. He returned all the ferocious beings to their destinations and headed towards his home with the princess. At this time he ran into a buffalo shepherd. The cock asked him to tell his mother to arrange for his wedding with the princess. The mother said, 'How can a cock marry a princess?' But she had to arrange the wedding. People had to believe the cock. He married the princess, and as he became a man at night, he enjoyed the company of the princess. One night, the princess looked for the cock's feathers and burnt them in the fire. The prince could not find his feathers even when he looked for them desperately. He had to stay a man from that time onwards. Both the prince and the princess passed time happily.

Prince Rama

There were once a king and a queen who did not have any children. After a long time, a son was born to them, and they named him Rama. The priest saw his horoscope and said he would die when he went to his *kohbar* room, the room where a bride and a bridegroom spend their first night, if he got married. The king said he would not have his son married, and his son therefore would not die.

The boy grew into a handsome young prince, and his mother wanted him to get married. The king insisted that Rama should not marry, but the queen did not listen to him. The wedding took place. Before visiting the *kohbar* room, Prince Rama said, 'If I die, please do not burn my body; just put it on a wooden bier.' When the prince went to his *kohbar* room and slept on the bed he never woke up.

The king took his son's dead body to a funeral place and left him on a wooden bier. The queen was disconsolate, and began blaming Rama's wife. The queen thought his wife's presence was ominous, and that she must have cast evil signs on the prince. The queen began to torture the princess, and the poor girl suffered quietly.

One day, a poor village woman who collected cow-dung came by and told the princess she had seen Rama hovering around the wooden bier. He was all by himself. Rama's wife did not believe her and thought it was a joke. The poor village woman asked her to go and see it herself. The princess went to that place and quietly sat under the *peepal* tree's trunk, hiding herself. She saw two fairies who came with two large metal plates full of sweets, and saw Prince Rama hovering around them. He sat on a cot near the fairies and asked them why they brought two metal plates. The fairies answered that one was for the prince and the other one was for his wife, who was hiding herself in the *peepal* trunk.

Rama looked for her and saw that she really was hiding beneath the tree. He asked her why had she come there, and what her trouble was. The princess said she was in great trouble. His mother tortured her a lot, and did not give her food. She related all her sufferings. Prince Rama asked her to go home and assured her that he would bring her food every night. The princess returned to her house. Rama came to his queen's room with food and goodies everyday, and they spent many happy hours together. They would chew and spit out *paan* (betel leaf).

The queen began claiming that Rama's wife was unchaste. Prince Rama's wife bore all this quietly, but she became pregnant. Her mother-in-law was furious with her: Her daughter-in-law had brought shame to the family.

When the ninth month passed, Lord Indra sent a fairy midwife to deliver the queen's baby. The mother-in-law could not believe her eyes and became very upset. The fairy midwife said, 'Why are you so furious and upset with your daughter-in-law?' 'Your son comes everyday.' She became more upset and thought this fairy was joking with her. Her son had died. How could he spend time with his wife? The mother was told that Prince Rama was Lord Indra's favorite mortal. 'If you don't trust me, watch him tonight, and you will trust me, said the fairy.' And in the night Prince Rama came and the mother happily embraced him. Prince Rama said to his mother, 'I am no longer your son, but my son will take my place. Consider him your son.'

Prince Rama said to his wife that if she wanted him to stay, then she should arrange for a *chhaThi* ceremony and invite Lord Indra with his fairies. If she pinched the baby three times, he said, and make him cry hard, then Lord Indra would ask her why the baby was crying. 'Give him a good reason', the prince said, and the fairies would tell Lord Indra that the father is Rama.

The day of *chhaThihaar*, a pomp-filled celebration on the sixth day after a child's birth, arrived. Lord Indra arrived with a lot of fairies and gifts and offerings. The king had made a lot of preparation for this auspicious occasion, and many people had come to bless the child. Prince Rama's wife pinched the child, and he started crying very hard and would not stop. Lord Indra naturally asked her why the child was crying. 'The baby wants his daddy', the fairies said. Lord Indra asked who the father was. The fairies answered that the father was Prince Rama. The Lord Indra ordered Rama back from the dead to stay with his wife and child. From then, on Rama lived happily with his parents and his wife and child.

A Carpenter and a Goldsmith

Once there was a carpenter and a goldsmith who were great friends. They lived together and would go places together. Both of them decided to earn some money, and got ready to travel. After traveling around, they earned a lot of money through carpentry and jewelry making. They decided to store their earned money together.

After some time, the two friends returned home. The money they had earned needed to be divided. They began to fight over it. The goldsmith wanted his share, while the carpenter wanted half of the entire earning. They decided to go to the king for a fair justice. The king listened to their exposition. He assured them he would be fair in his judgment, but they had to show him their workmanship at carpentry and jewelry making. The king said, 'As soon as I see your skills, I will be able to come to a fair judgment.' The goldsmith requested the king to get a large pond dug, and also asked for some gold; the king did these things. The goldsmith made a large gold fish and let it float in the pond. It was quite a beautiful sight. People watched the fish and were very happy.

Now it was the carpenter's turn. The king asked him to show his skill. He asked for wood and he got it right away. He made a beautiful horse and asked for someone who could ride the horse. No one was willing to ride the horse. The king became disappointed and promised to give half of his kingdom whoever would ride that horse. Still no one rode the horse. Finally the king's son got ready to ride the horse. When he got on the horse, the carpenter pushed a button and the king's son began to fly on the horse. But the carpenter didn't show him how to stop the horse.

The king's son flew very far on that horse. Suddenly his

finger by chance pressed a button and the horse stopped. He got down in another city. The king of that city had a daughter. She was attracted to the prince and wanted to marry him. He married the princess, and after a year the princess got pregnant. He returned to his own village with her. On the way the princess said she was not feeling well and asked him to stop the horse. They wanted to get off the horse, but the prince saw water all over and no dry land was visible. Finally, there was a small hillock on which he stopped the horse. The princess got down and delivered a baby boy. The prince flew his horse to fetch a midwife. He tied his horse in a place and went looking for a midwife. When he returned with a midwife he did not find the horse. The horse had disappeared. A shepherd had broken it into pieces. The midwife returned to her house and the prince had no choice but to stay in that village. He began to work as a householder.

Elsewhere, the princess somehow raised the son by herself. Her son was playing when a merchant passed by and saw the princess and her son. The merchant called the princess his daughter and took her to his house along with her handsome son. They began to live there with the merchant. After a few months she said to the merchant that she would like to go on a pilgrimage. She left the boy with the merchant. The boatman took the princess in his boat and stopped at the same place where the wooden horse had broken. The princess recognized the place and made an announcement to the people there that whoever could relate the story of the wooden horse would marry her. No one knew about the story of the horse, and no one came to marry her. But when her real husband heard the announcement, he was able to relate the story of his wooden horse.

The princess came to the merchant's house with her real husband. After their short stay with the merchant, the princess decided to return to her real home with the prince and her son. They arrived at their home and their fathers were overjoyed to see them. The prince told his father the entire story. The king heard the entire story and came to the following conclusion: The carpenter and the goldsmith both worked hard and were good with their skills. They could divide the money into half. Both of them did accordingly and returned home.

The King's Daughter-Dove

There was a king. He was very poor. He had no children, and thought he should do something about it. The king and his queen talked about it constantly. At this very time, the queen's sister-in-law came and asked them what they had been talking about so much. The king told her that they did not have children so they were thinking of a solution. The sister-in-law suggested they should visit a great saint who lived near her house. He could solve their problem. The king and the queen got into many arguments and did not know who should see the saint. After a lot of arguments, they finally decided that both of them should go see the saint. The sister-in-law joined them on the visit. The three of them left together to look for the place.

Eventually, they arrived at the hut of that sage. All of them started relating their problems to him. The saint said, 'After nine months the queen will deliver a birdie. This will be the answer to all of your problems.' All of them came back to their house and began to live waiting for this occasion. In nine months the queen delivered a baby dove. The king summoned the midwife and told her not to tell anybody that the queen had delivered a dove. She should tell everyone she had delivered a baby girl.

The day arrived when all the women and children of the neighborhood assembled to see and bathe the newly born baby-girl. This was a ritual ceremony. Every newly born baby was given a bath that day before the women folk of the kingdom. The king announced to his assembled guests that the newly born baby girl would remain and bathe in her room—no one would see her because hers had been a difficult birth.

She needed to be saved lest she fall victim to the evil eye. The girl would be kept in a cage, and she would not be taken out for twelve years. To avert the evil eye, a black earthen pot would be placed in her room. People thought and agreed that the child should be saved from the evil eye. She needed a lot of protection.

Six months passed, and the king started getting worried about his daughter's wedding. The marriage got settled. During the wedding, the girl's face was not shown to anybody. The king announced to the people that the girl had to be kept in a cage so that no evil eye was cast on her. The girl was sent to her husband in the cage. Her mother-in-law saw that the cage was closed, and could not see her daughter-in-law's face. When she asked for the reason, she got the same answer about the evil eye.

After quite some time the mother-in-law opened the cage, and saw that there was only a dove in the cage. The entire husband's family became very furious. They left the bird alone and went to a distant land. When the dove found herself alone in the entire house, she tried to live her life nicely. She tied a pitcher to her neck and went to the pond to bring water. She filled the pitcher with water and brought it home. She washed the entire floor of the house and cleaned it. And she began to enjoy the clean house and started living well.

The village people found the latch of the door always closed. They thought that this was because there was no one in the house. In fact, there was only a dove in the closed house. But this dove used to get transformed into a twelve-year old girl every night.

In this way a few days went by. One day, the dove was filling her pitcher with water at the pond. Lord Shiva and the goddess Parvati happened to pass by from the same route. Parvati saw the dove. She understood her whole story and felt great pity on the dove. She requested Lord Shiva to transform the dove into a girl, because the dove had all the feminine qualities. Lord Shiva got quite upset with the goddess, but the goddess insisted on it and Lord Shiva had no choice. After much insistence, Lord Shiva transformed the dove into a girl. From that day, the dove (in the form of a girl) began to live in that house. After some time, when the girl's in-laws returned and came to their house, they saw the dove changed into a girl. They were overjoyed with her and lived a happy life.

The Prince Destined to be Short-lived

A great king was very wealthy but he had no children who could benefit from his wealth. As he was desperate, he set fire to his palace. The smoke reached Lord Indra's *Indrasan* and shook it up. Lord Indra thought that the king was performing a *yagya* (sacrifice ritual). He came and asked, 'Please open the door. Why are you burning so much wealth?' The king answered, 'I loved my wealth, but there is no one to use it.' The Lord said, 'You will have a son. Whenever you see a bunch of twelve bananas, hit it with your left hand and catch the bananas with your right hand. Bring it and feed it to the queen. She will deliver a baby boy after nine months. But the son will live for twelve years only and after that he will die.'

The king fed the bananas to the queen. After nine months, the queen gave birth to a son. The king raised him with pomp and grandeur, and educated him. The prince grew up into an elegant young man.

Twelve years passed, and the time of his death arrived. The prince said to his parents that he would go out of his palace. He went to a jungle. The king and the queen kept crying and lost their sight. The prince sat under a tree in the forest and began to cry. Lord Shiva and Parvati were passing by. The goddess heard someone crying. She requested Lord Shiva to look for whoever was crying so much, and to find out what the reason for all those tears was. Lord Shiva said they would not go looking for the crier. There might not be any reason for him to cry. But Goddess Parvati insisted, as usual, and was willing to go look for him by herself.

Finally, both went and found him together. They asked the prince why he was crying. The prince said he was going to die right away. That was the cause for his crying. Both of them waited. They saw the ghosts who came to take his life. Lord Shiva and Parvati began to beat them. God Almighty realized that a boy would not die right then, even though he was destined to die. So he made the prince very thirsty. The prince went to a well to drink water. He was going to sink in the well but Lord Shiva and Parvati caught him and saved him from dying. So God Almighty thought of another way of taking the life of the prince. He created strong sunlight. Because of the intense heat, the prince sat under a tree in the shade. But the tree started breaking on him. Again Lord Shiva and Parvati saved him, catching hold of the trunk as it fell.

God Almighty started devising more and more complicated plans to somehow take the life of the prince. He thought of getting him married. As he would be in a canopy for the wedding ceremony, a scorpion would bite him. So the marriage was arranged, and the prince sat in the canopy to get married. A scorpion came crawling on his foot, Lord Shiva started warning the prince: 'Oh child, remove your foot.' He did so and killed the scorpion.

God Almighty thought of sending a ferocious snake in his *kohbar*. The snake would bite him and he would die. But again, Lord Shiva and Parvati intervened and killed the snake. By this time, the death period that fate appointed to the prince had whiled away.

Having survived his wedding night, the prince asked his father-in-law to do the ceremony of *roksadi* (the wedding ceremony when the bride leaves her house and goes to the bridegroom's house). So the prince departed with his bride and arrived at his own palace. The children who were his childhood friends ran and announced their arrival to the king and the queen, his father and mother. They did not believe their son's friends, because they thought their son had died long time ago. But when he arrived at the door, they turned their heads towards the sound of his voice, and their lost vision came back. They could see now with their eyes. They saw their son and his bride, and they were overjoyed. They thanked Lord Shiva and Parvati for thwarting their son's fate and saving him from an early death. They built a very beautiful temple to Lord Shiva and Goddess Parvati, and began to worship there daily.

A Wrestler Prince

Once there was a king who had only one son. There was no dearth of food for the prince, so he ate a lot of food, and turned out to be an athlete. He was a champion wrestler, and with his club, he could kill almost any number of animals. One day, an intoxicated elephant started attacking people. The wrestler prince killed him in no time. The prince had a beautiful garden that he adored. He loved going to the garden, relaxing there, and even sleeping there quite often.

One day when he was sleeping in his garden, a lot of sheep came in, led by their shepherd. The prince (who by then had become a king) warned the shepherd, and threatened to kill all his sheep. The shepherd did not listen to the prince and said rudely that the prince could not dare kill his sheep. The king brought his club and wielded it, killing all the sheep. The heads of all sheep and their shepherd were severed. All the shepherds gathered and invited seven hundred demon giants the same night to kill the prince. The wife of the prince came to know about this and asked her husband not to go anywhere that night. The king assured her that he would be back in no time. He went to the garden.

In the garden he placed a box and covered it with sheets. It gave the impression that someone was sleeping under the sheet. The king himself climbed up a mango tree and sat there quietly. The giants came in the night, and they were bent on eating the king up. When they removed the sheets they found only an empty box. The furious giants started tearing the sheets apart. The king from the top of the tree threw his club and chopped off the heads of all the giants.

In the morning the shepherds heard that the king had killed all of the giants. They became even more determined to kill the king somehow. They invited ferocious tigers this time, and they were absolutely certain that the famous tigers would kill the king. The queen found out about the ferocious tigers, and did not want to send the king to the garden at any cost. But the king with great difficulty came to the garden. He did the same thing as he had done earlier. He covered the box with the sheets and made it look as if a man was sleeping under the sheets. He himself climbed up the mango tree. All the tigers arrived, and the king threw his mighty club and killed them all, despite their ferocity. The king never got killed, and all the efforts of the shepherds failed.

Princess Belmanti

There were once four brothers. When their father and mother died, the four brothers thought of going to another city to earn livelihood. Three brothers were married at that time, but the youngest was still unmarried. While leaving home, all three brothers explained to their wives that they should look after the youngest brother nicely. The three sisters-in-law started taking very good care of this brother, but they each began badgering him to marry their younger sisters. They became very insistent, and the poor boy got ready to leave the house. The sisters-in-law became very offended with him. All three said sarcastically, 'Our sisters are obviously not good enough for you, so we will watch you marry the great Princess Belmanti.' Princess Belmanti was a legendary, famous beauty in the area, and she was known for attracting crowds of bachelors, all ready to die over her.

The youngest brother got out in search of the princess Belmanti. As he was walking around, he entered a jungle where he found a hut of a hermit saint. He cleaned the hut and its entrance, and prepared cannabis for the saint to smoke. When the saint woke up he saw the clean hut and the cannabis. 'Who could do all this for me?' he thought. He looked all over and saw a boy. He called him and asked him what he wanted. The boy said he wanted to marry the famous princess Belmanti. The saint said, 'Go straight and in the way you will find a *bel* tree (wood apple tree). It will have only one wood apple fruit. Pluck the fruit and bring it to me. But don't, by any chance, look back. If you do, you will burn into ashes.'

The boy plucked the fruit and happened to look back. As soon as he did, he was burnt to ashes. The saint was waiting for the boy desperately. But he never showed up. The saint finally came looking for him, and saw he had been burnt to ashes. The saint picked up the ashes and blew at them, and the boy woke up alive. This time the saint warned him not to look back at any cost. He went there again and plucked another fruit and brought it and did not turn back. The saint asked him to take the wood apple fruit home, and to break it twice.

The boy prepared to come home with the fruit. In the way when he arrived near his home he felt thirsty. So he sat near a well, and prepared to drink water. As he reached toward the well, the fruit dropped and broke. From that fruit, the princess Belmanti came out, all dressed up with expensive jewelry and clothes. The boy went to the village to get a carriage and a palanquin. In the meantime the princess felt thirsty. At this very time, a midwife had come to the same well to fetch water. The princess asked her for water then the midwife gave her the bucket to fetch water herself. When the princess was trying to fetch water, the midwife took her clothes and jewelry and pushed her in the well. She herself wore those precious jewelry and clothes and waited for the boy wrapped in the princess's clothes. When the boy came back with a carriage and palanquin, the midwife sat on it. The boy thought she was the princess, and took her to his home.

The preparation for the wedding took place in his hometown. In their preparations for the wedding, one day all the four brothers were going and stopped at the well to drink water. When the oldest brother put a bucket to fetch water from the well, he saw an extraordinarily beautiful flower. He was not able to retrieve the flower in spite of his efforts. All three brothers tried their best to fetch the flower, but were not successful. At last the youngest brother put the bucket into the well, and the flower jumped into the bucket.

They came home and gave the midwife the flower. She recoiled when she saw it, and she threw it on ashes. Flowers and leaves grew on the ashes. The midwife threw away the flowers again. This time, a wood apple tree sprouted overnight from the ashes. The horrified midwife took the tree and gave it to a gardener. The gardener who took the fruit plant and said he would give half of the fruits to them. Only one fruit grew, however, and the boy asked the gardener to give it to him. 'When it grows again, then you can reap it', he told the gardener, who turned the fruit over to him. When the boy broke the fruit (*bel*), princess Belmanti came out of it. The midwife was buried alive, and the princess married the boy. Even though it was uttered in sarcasm that the boy should marry the princess Belmanti, it came true after great hardship. Thus, man should try hard to fulfill his wishes.

Lord Shiva's Blessing

There was a king of a western country who was married, but who wished to marry a very beautiful girl in addition to his first wife. So he went to an eastern region. He went quite far and began to practice religious austerity. He performed *puja* for quite some time, and at one point, his first wife sent a crow to tell him that she in his absence was dying. Even then, the king's heart did not melt, and he said he would not do anything unless he got married again. He kept doing *puja* until one day he went to sleep, and a princess—the daughter of the king of that country—arrived and attempted to wake him up. When the king did not wake up, then the princess wrote a note on his sheet about how he had rebuffed her and left.

When the king woke up then he read what was written on the sheet. He was very hurt and mortified, so he cut his body into two parts with his sword. In the evening Lord Shiva and his wife Goddess Parvati were out for a walk. Parvati told the Lord Shiva that this king had performed a lot of austerities, and that until he revived him, she would not budge from that spot. Lord Shiva listened to Parvati, joined the two parts of the king's body, and sprinkled him with a few drops of nectar. The king woke up alive.

The king went in search of the princess who had visited him. He went to the princess's father and asked him for his daughter's hand in marriage. When the princess's father did not agree to marry his daughter to the king, the king declared he was ready for war.

The two started fighting. The king, however, was alone and could not have continued fighting against the princess's father. So he remembered how Lord Shiva had come to his aid, and called on him. Lord Shiva appeared with his army of ghosts, who engaged in a lot of fighting with the princess's father and his army. The army of ghosts nearly vanquished the princess's father, who agreed to marry his daughter off to the king.

After their wedding, the king decided to take her to his homeland. The king became excessively proud, and believed that there was no other girl prettier than his wife. There was a huge river along their route to his homeland. While they crossed the river, they faced a terrible storm and rain and his boat sank. In the river, the king happened to see a water princess. He almost fainted when he saw her. When he came to his senses, then he found out that the water princess had fallen in love with him. The king married her and began to live there, by the river. His second wife stayed with him there, up on the banks.

After some time, he thought again of his homeland and wanted to go back there. They all were preparing to leave when the river ebbed towards the king and threw him a bracelet and a peacock. They sat on the peacock, which flew them to the king's palace. On their return, all three wives and the king began to live happily because of Lord Shiva's blessings. All the king's wishes were fulfilled because he had done a lot of religious austerities for Lord Shiva.

A Princess and Her Husband, a Gram Picker

There was a king and he had seven daughters. The king adored his younger daughter, who had been his pet since she was born. One day the king called all his seven daughters and asked them, 'Tell me truly, whose fortune you are living by?' The six eldest daughters answered, 'Dear daddy, we are living by the grace of your fortune.' However, the youngest one answered, 'I am living and thriving on the basis of my own destiny.' The king was very hurt. He got very mad with his youngest daughter, so, though he married his six daughters off to royal families, he married his seventh daughter off to a very poor gram picker. All six daughters went to their husbands' homes and began to live happily.

The youngest princess went to her husband's home also. He was very poor and his livelihood depended on his gram and grain picking. He would roam around all day picking grain, and then in the evening he would cook some food to survive. One day her husband came home with two large yellow stones. When his wife looked at them, she asked him where he got these gold stones, for she recognized that they were actually real gold. The poor fellow said he got them from a great saint. The saint had said to him, 'Give these stones to your wife.' After hearing this story, the wife said, 'Go and get four or five more stones.'

The gram picker brought quite a few stones to her. His wife got a very beautiful palace built by selling those gold stones. When the palace was fully built then the princess arranged for a very large sacrificial ceremony in her mansion. She invited all the great, neighboring kings and had all various kinds of good food served for them. She sat them in a row to serve them food. It turned out that her dear father was also sitting in the same row. All the cooks and servants served the food to the royal kings, but the princess herself went to her father again and again and served him food with her own hand.

The father started wondering who this princess was. The king could not figure out why this princess would come to him and serve him food herself. He asked the princess, 'Oh, princess! Would you let me meet your king? I want to see this great king.' The princess then said, 'Daddy, you don't recognize me! I am your youngest daughter and the king is the gram picker, husband and your son-in-law.' The king saw him, and then realized that this person was in reality the same poor gram picker, though he now looked like a very handsome prince.

The king became very happy. He said to the princess, 'My daughter, you had truly said that everyone lives and thrives by the grace of his own destiny.' He repented his mistake and took them to his own royal palace with great respect, where he presented them to all his subjects, and to all of his other daughters and their husbands. Everyone lived in his palace happily thereafter.

The Co-wives' Jealousy

There was a king who married six times in an effort to have a child, but he did not have any. Finally he got married one more time. Fortunately, the newest wife of his got pregnant. But when his first six wives came to know this, they believed the new wife would not let them stay in the palace. They started finding fault with the pregnant wife, and they got her turned out of the house by the king. The youngest queen was grief stricken. She began begging, and began to like her new life. A son was born to her, and the young queen somehow began to raise him.

He grew up into a young man then he wanted to go around to earn money and live his life. His mother said to him, 'You can go east, you can go west, you can go north, but do not go south.' The son heard this and wanted to know the reason for it. The mother did not want to tell him, but finally she said, 'In the south your father rules over his kingdom. There your father has six queens. They are my co-wives. If they come to know you they will kill you.' Hearing this he immediately decided to go south and didn't listen to his mother. He accepted a job in his father's palace. After some time, the six queens came to know that he was the son of the youngest queen. They thought if the king happened to find this out, then he would turn the six queens out and would keep his son in his palace instead. So they talked to the king against the boy and got him tied up. After a long time his mother came crying and looking for him.

She cried so much that even the trees and shrubs around her started withering. When she found out that her son was tied up in the king's palace then she went to the back of the palace and started crying. One day, the king heard her crying and he sent his servant for her. The servant asked her, 'Why are you crying? Who are you? Are you a goddess or a witch or a fairy? What is your sorrow, that you have come here to cry like this?' The mother kept crying in spite of the questions. The king heard her again and came to her himself. He also asked her who she was and why she was crying so bitterly. Then the queen said that the king had tied her son who came to work in his palace. The king wanted to hear more from her and she told him all about herself and her story. She was pregnant and her six co-wives got her out of the palace. The queen had somehow raised the son on her own, and lived by begging to support him.

When the king heard all this, he became restless for his son. He turned his six queens out and made them paupers. The king brought the youngest queen to his palace and his son lived like a prince and later became the king.

The Brahmin's Story

There was a Brahmin who lived in a village. He had only one son. After some time, the father died and the son finished his funeral rites and began to live his life. The mother and the son began to fight after a few days. The boy was hurt and began to run away. He would not stop in spite of his mother's persuasive calls to forget their arguments and stay at home.

As he was running he met an old man. The old man wanted to know why he was running away. Why was he doing this, and who would take up his hereditary position of priest? The boy answered he did not want to do that work. He felt like studying. The old man said he should study with someone of his own caste, and not with just anyone. The boy went to several schools to study but he could not find anyone of his own caste. Eventually, during his travels, the boy, who had been married at a very young age, arrived at his father-in-law's house, although he was unaware of this fact. His father-in-law used to teach, and the boy decided to remain and study there from that day forward. From that day he began to study there. His *guru* also fed and sheltered him.

There was a king's son who also studied at the school. One day, the prince saw the *guru's* daughter bringing food; he wanted to marry that girl, and told his parents all about this. His father told everything about his son to his *guru*. The *guru* agreed to marry the prince to the girl, believing this match to be more advantageous than the one he had made so long ago with a faraway Brahmin's son. But the girl herself stipulated one condition that the prince had to fulfill. The girl said that the prince should build a gold house that would be large enough to be his home, and he should also build a cloth house in the middle of a pond. Only then would she marry the prince. The prince got everything ready. The date of the wedding was also finalized, and was set to take place in the cloth house. At this time the girl said to the prince, 'If you are righteous, then please throw a handful of ritual kindling in the pond. If it burns then I will marry you.' The prince did exactly what she had said but it didn't burn, because the girl was chaste and had asked him to perform an impossible task knowing her marriage had been arranged long before. Thus, the marriage with the prince did not take place.

The girl came back to her house, and her parents decided they should honor the prearranged marriage. The boy who had come to study returned home, and soon after the girl left her parent's house and headed towards her husband's house. When she came to the boy's house, then, though the wedding rites were performed, the boy believed the girl had also been married to the prince, and so never ate food cooked by her.

The boy studied hard and became a *pundit* (priest). One day, he went to his client to do the regular recitation of the sacred text, which was scheduled to take nine days. At this time, his wife came in disguise and stayed in the garden of that village. She also asked him to do recitation of the sacred text. The *pundit* didn't recognize her, though she was his own wife. When the recitation was over, then his wife fed him pigeon's meat on some excuse.

When the *pundit* came home and the occasion arose for his dinnertime, he refused to eat. The girl said, 'I am not worse than that girl who fed you pigeon's meat.' The *pundit* was very surprised and realized that it was his wife who had fed him pigeon's meat. From then onwards he started eating food cooked by his wife and they lived happily.

Gold is Like Dirt

There was a king who did not have any kingly qualifications. He spent all his time thinking of wealth. He would collect revenue taxes from his public and go on filling his treasury with wealth. Sometimes he would fight with weaker kings and defeat them in order to loot their gold and wealth. His treasury was filled to the brim with gold and silver.

In his kingdom there lived a cobbler. He used to make two pairs of shoes everyday. He used to sell one pair a day and manage to feed his family of eight people somehow. His shoes were very nice. Poor people and also saints and ascetics who did not have shoes would go to him to get shoes. Sometimes he had to give away both pairs of shoes he had made that day without receiving any money, and he and his family used to starve.

By chance, the cobbler and the king (after getting old) died the same day. When the king died, death's messenger came and dragged the body away. But at the cobbler's bedside, the lord of death himself came, brought a throne, and asked the cobbler to sit on it in order to go to heaven. The cobbler said that his king also should sit on the throne and go with him. Then the lord of death said that he did not discriminate between king or subject, poor or rich, low caste or high caste. Death explained that merit was earned only by action, and what one had accomplished in his life; man was rewarded accordingly, and got whatever fruit he deserved. If the king's treasury is full of gold and silver, then he does not sit on death throne.

The cobbler had a lot of compassion when he saw the king being dragged by death's messenger and crying. So he said to the lord of death that he would not go to heaven unless the king sat on the throne with him. The lord said, 'No one goes to heaven because of wealth. If you want the king to go with you, then you give the king half of your earned merits (results of good deeds).' The cobbler agreed. Right away lord Chitragupta was called, and half of the cobbler's earnings were given to the king. After that the king and the cobbler sat on the throne together and went to heaven. It is rightly said that if one's actions are not morally correct, then all the gold in the world is like dirt.

Lorikayan

Lorik was a handsome well-built young man, and so was his younger brother Samar. Their old mother Khulni was worried about her sons' weddings. One day she said to her old husband Kubja Sardar, 'Our sons are of marriageable age. They should get married now.' The father sent a letter to the son's *guru* Mitrajal with the barber about their wedding. The *guru* answered, 'Everything will take place by the grace of Devi (goddess).'

The time came when, in the village Aghori, the barber and a Brahmin decided upon and fixed the marriage of Lorik and Manjari. The wedding day drew near. The question arose of how Lorik, who was very poor, was arranged to marry Manjari, the daughter of a king! The *guru* gave his assurance: 'Everything will be alright by the grace of Devi.' The bridegroom's procession (the *baaraat*) came at the right time. On the way, Lorik and his *guru* fought with a washer man to obtain the king's outfit, and also got a lot of jewelry of gold and silver from a goldsmith. The groom's procession proceeded to Aghori village with pomp and grandeur, and the wedding of Lorik and Manjari took place. A lot of prominent fighters came to the *mandap*, but Lorik defeated all of them.

Lorik and Manjari arrived with a lot of wealth in Gaura Gujarat, Lorik's village. When Chandwa heard the wedding drums, she couldn't control herself. Chandwa was the daughter of Gaura Gujarat's king, Sahdev. She was very much attracted to Lorik. She, on the advice of her maid, came to Lorik's house with a lot of diamonds and pearls to do the ceremony of *chumavan* (greeting ritual). In doing the greeting ceremony, she pinched Lorik's cheeks and Lorik also became attracted to her. Chandwa returned to her house after squandering a lot of jewels, and Lorik came to know from his mother that Chandwa was the daughter of King Sahdev of Gaura Gujarat.

Khulni used to feed her sons a lot of milk, as they were *ahirs* (milkman). Then they used to go to their *guru* for their work-out, after which they also drank a lot of milk. Only then would they come back to their house. On the way somehow Chandwa asked Lorik to come to her house and expressed her love to Lorik. Lorik said to Chandwa, 'You are the wife of Malsaudhara, so why are you attracted to me?' Chandwa answered, 'He is impotent. I have chosen you to be my husband.'

Finally, Lorik agreed to elope with her to Hardibazaar. Khulni, Manjari, and her sister LuRhki, who had also chosen Lorik her husband, all came to know about this. They intended to stand guard all night, but they fell asleep through Devi's grace. Thus, Lorik and Chandwa did not have any problem running away into the night. He arrived in Devithan with Chandwa and from there they were to go to Hardibazaar. Along the way Lorik had to fight with boatmen and some tribal men; after defeating them he arrived Hardibazaar.

In Hardibazaar, a Chhattu merchant accepted Lorik as his son and Chandwa as his daughter-in-law, and gave them shelter in his house. The king there made Lorik the collector of revenue of Jamunighat. Lorik became adept at collecting full revenue, and the king was very happy with him.

In Gaura Gujarat, however, there was turmoil. The King Sahdev started torturing Lorik's family. After a while, Lorik's brother Samar collected one lakh cows with horns and went to neighboring Paali-pipari and began to graze them there. An ox called Birna and a bird called Baadril joined Samar. They asked Samar not to continue grazing his cows in this town because of inauspicious signals. But Samar did not listen. He tied them and said they could be free only if Manjari remembered to untie them. Then he went to Paali-pipari with his cows, where he got killed after fighting with the tribal Kols. The Kols captured all the cows, but the cows let Samar flowaway from Paali-pipari on stream of their milk. They helped Samar reach his wife's home, where she became *satee* with her husband Samar.

When this news reached Gaura, there was uproar of sorrow. King Sahdev gave orders that this news should never reach Hardibazaar, where Lorik was. Eventually, however, Manjari remembered Birna the ox and the bird Badril, and they magically freed themselves from the tie and came to her. The bird flew to Hardibazaar with Manjari's letter and gave it to Lorik. Lorik, crying, arrived in Gaura in disguise with Chandwa and his newly born son Chandrajit. He tested Manjari's virtue, and she convinced him that she had been faithful. Manjari welcomed Chandwa as if she were her own sister. Chandwa's father also accepted them and married them with pomp and grandeur. After getting his *guru's* permission, Lorik arrived at Pali-pipari. There, he defeated the Kols with his valor and freed the lakhs of cows they had taken. He returned to his village with grandeur. Lorik became the king of Gaura and Pali-pipari and lived happily with his family.

Gopichand

King Gopichand wanted to attain asceticism, so he dressed in rags and began to go towards a forest. His mother Nainavati grabbed his rags and stood by him. She said, 'Son, I bore you for nine months in my belly. If you had died right after birth I would have endured it, but I cannot bear losing a full-grown, living son.' Gopichand said, 'Mother, you should imagine that my departure means that you have always been a barren woman.' The mother answered, 'How could that be possible? You cannot desert your household. First pay for the milk I gave you—only then can you become an ascetic.' Gopichand said, 'No man has yet been born who can count all the stars in the sky, and no man will ever be born who can repay the cost of his mother's milk.' Finally, his crying mother said 'Alright, son, go. Be alive and live as an ascetic in the world. Go beg in the three regions that neighbor this kingdom, but never go to your sister Birna's country. Your sister will cry for six months if she learns what you are doing. She had hopes that the home of her childhood would flourish, but you have shattered these hopes by forsaking your kingdom.'

Gopichand left everything. He left his elephants, his camels, his nine hundred soldiers, and five hundred crying unmarried girls and nine hundred lamenting married women. Mother Nainavati sat at his throne and began to cry. Birds and geese began to cry on the roofs. The village cultivators, the travelers, and the women who drew water from wells all began to cry. 'Oh, my god,' they said, 'how can our loving, benevolent king be forsaking us and become an ascetic?'

Gopichand kept walking, and he arrived in a banana forest as evening fell. The greenery of the forest and the deer all began to cry. The trees and shrubs in this dense forest had pity on him. They themselves became geese and made him a parrot. Then they flew with him to his sister's country. There, smeared with ashes and in the guise of a saint, he began to wander around, asking for the king's address. The beautiful women of that city said, 'There will be high ceiling and low door. The door's threshold will be of gold and silver. At the entrance, there will be a dry, twelve-year-old sandal tree. That is the king's house.'

At his sister's door, Gopichand sat lighting a penance fire. The twelve-year-old dry sandal tree became green. The king and the subjects of that city were amazed at this. The old maid Munga told Queen Birna, and she came to Gopichand, who invited him to dinner. Gopichand answered, 'I will eat a dinner cooked by a Brahmin priest.' She agreed, but that night everyone forgot to feed him. Gopichand said that if his sister ate, then there would be pudding for her, but in the storeroom everything would burn. After this, he played his flute. The sister listened. She summoned the Brahmin, who went to the storeroom and saw hundreds of dishes burning. Then Munga came to him with dry fruits. Gopichand became angry, and all the four directions became dark. He saw the food and laughed in the darkness. Then the night changed into daylight. On five leaf plates, there appeared ashes of penance and that changed into food.

Early in the morning on the next day, Gopichand came to the river to bathe. He was hiding his body lest his sister recognize him. But his thirty-two teeth started shining in the water, and his beauty increased eight times more until his form sparkled from below the surface of the river. Everyone was puzzled to see this unique saint.

After he bathed, he went to his sister's door to beg. Then the maid Munga said to the queen, 'This saint resembles your brother, Gopichand.' The sister replied, 'May you go to doom. When my brother comes, it will be with royal magnificence, and the entire city will be awestruck.' After this Birna came with all her maids to give the beggar alms. She said, 'Baba, saint, take these alms and leave my door.' Gopichand said, 'I have quit my mother's palace because I believe wealth and riches are worth no more than rocks and stones.' The sister said, 'I give you gold and silver and you consider them rock and stone. If I give you a stole, you would make it into a rag. You have taken an oath to forsake the world, so leave my door. I don't have clothes or riches worthy of you.'

Gopichand replied, 'So much conceit because of your wealth! You do not recognize even your own brother.' Birna said, 'I will be able to recognize you only when you show me the symbols of my childhood home.' Gopichand told her, 'In your hand you have your father's ring, on your body you have mother's colorful clothes and on your wrist you have our sister-in-law's bracelet.' Now the sister grabbed his rag and began to cry. 'Oh, my God, you have forsaken our mother and your kingdom! Return to her, reclaim your throne, and I will give all the wealth in the world.' Gopichand would not agree to Birna's desperate pleas. His sister died in distress.

Gopichand repented when he saw his sister's lifeless body. 'Let me also die here,' he cried. At this very moment, God appeared in the guise of a Brahmin and said, 'You have nectar in your little finger. Make your sister drink it, and she will revive. You yourself can remain an ascetic in the guise of a large black bee.' Gopichand did what the Brahmin told him, and his sister jolted to life again. Then, however, she started crying and running from one street to another. She reached the sandal tree, held fast to it, and sobbed. The sandal tree said, 'Why are you crying? Your brother has become a saint.' Birna could not bear the thought of her mother alone and forsaken, and continued to sob. The earth tore apart and she entered into its mighty cleft, forever severing the relationship between brother and sister.

Resama

Resama was the sister of the zamindar Ajabi Singh of Mokamah in the state of Bihar. She was exquisitely pretty, and it became difficult to find a suitable husband for her. She was attracted to her brother's dear friend Virmal Chuharmal. He was bright, gallant, and very handsome. Resama wanted to see him and to somehow express her love to him. She began to look for ways to sneak out of her home. She asked permission to go to the Tulsiram well, but was not allowed. Finally, she dressed herself up very beautifully, climbed out the window, and traveled to the well.

The well was along the path to the *chaaraadih* wrestling place, where Virmal Chuharmal lived. He used to come by the same path and drink water at that well, and that day, he arrived there not too long after Resama. Resama thanked the Goddess for sending him so quickly. Then she asked Virmal, 'Traveler, where is your house? What is your name?' Virmal introduced himself to her. Then Resama pulled her veil off and said, 'Let us go to my house—I will give you water there. My beauty and these exquisite clothes—everything is for you. Let us fall in love with each other.' Virmal became very angry. He said, 'I have passed along this wrestlers' path for twelve years, and no one ever stopped me along this path to say something so inappropriate. You are my friend's sister, and therefore you are also related to me as a sister. Furthermore, you belong to an upper class family, and I come from much lower class family. It will be best for you to return to your house soon. Otherwise, if you are found, your head will be chopped off.' Resama replied, crying, 'No! If you will not accept me, then I will get your head chopped off.'

After this, in an ugly disguise, she went to her brother's court and complained that Virmal had subjected dishonor on her. At first Ajabi Singh could not believe this, but Resama cried and cried, and finally he had to trust her. She said, 'Do not kill Virmal, just tie him up and bring him here. I myself will punish him.' The commander of Ajabi Singh's seven hundred strong army was a man named Baandhiram, who also happened to be Virmal's uncle. He could not believe his nephew's misconduct. Still, he went to fight Virmal with Ajabi Singh and his huge army. At home, Resama prayed to the Goddess that, at any cost, Virmal would get caught, and that she could then somehow persuade him to marry her.

At the same time, Virmal was also offering prayers to the Devi. Devi herself appeared before Virmal and said, 'My son, here take sword and fight with this. Do not worry.' The fighting began. On one side fought Ajabi Singh, Baandhiram and the huge army they commanded, and on the other side Virmal fought alone with the Devi's sword. Ajabi Singh's entire army was killed. He was defeated, and he left the battleground. After this defeat, Baandhiram said to Ajabi Singh, 'I won't work in your palace. My nephew Virmal is a virtuous and great devotee of Devi. That is why he won the entire battle alone.' After this, Ajabi Singh came to his house and Resama again began harassing him. This goading aroused his passion, and he went to fight with even bigger army. The entire army got killed again. This time, Ajabi Singh was also among the casualties. Virmal embraced Ajabi Singh's chopped-off head, and cried out, 'Oh God, I had to cut my friend's head because of Resama!' After this he himself floated his friend's head down in the river Ganges.

In the city of Mokamah, people were grief-stricken. Ajabi Singh's mother cursed Resama and died from the sorrow of her son's death. And yes Resama still had not gained any wisdom. She asked another previous lover, Daljit Singh, to fight against Virmal with a big army. He, too, perished with his huge army.

Resama had run out of men to mount battles for her. She turned to Jirva, the betel-seller, and a woman who was extremely close to Virmal. She asked, 'How come Virmal visits you everyday and sits with you?' She answered, 'I was also once madly in love with him. But he always called me his sister. Once I accepted him as my brother, he never left my side. If you also accept him as your brother and act like his sister, he will never leave you.' But Resama did not like this solution. She left Jirva's home crying.

In the morning Resama heard the announcement that Virmal Chuharmal would opt for saintly entombment instead of continued battle. Resama, grief-stricken, came to the entombment and said, 'Oh God, if my love for him is true, then let my life end this very moment.' She kept taking Lord Rama's name, and finally he heard her prayer. She died right then and there. After this, a voice came from within Virmal's tomb, and said 'Worship my sister Resama before you worship me.' From then onwards, Resama and Virmal Chuharmal have always been worshipped together, the unwilling sister before the Devi's steadfast devotee.

Chhatri Ghughulia

Randpal Singh, the king of Jhajhampur, was considered brilliant, glorious and gallant. He was married in Ghatampur, and he had seven brothers-in-law who were called Ghatams. These Ghatams were big businessmen. At their place, seven hundred bulls were used for loading purposes everyday.

Once Raajaa Rampal Singh saw these bulls staggering through his kingdom, overloaded with the Ghatams' goods, and he got very angry. He made all the businessmen unload their goods and make lighter loads. This news went to the Ghatams. They decided to take revenge. The Holi festival of colors came. The Ghatams sent an invitation card to king Rampal with Gangu Barber. Randpal Singh's wife Yashoda, who was pregnant, understood the meaning behind it right away. She cried and tried her best to stop Randpal Singh from going to her brothers' home, but he did not listen to her. He wore his iron outfit and tied fifty-six daggers to his back. Then he sat atop his man-eating haikal horse and rode to Ghatampur. The wretched Ghatams wanted to kill him, and tried many ways, but every time he would worship Devi and was saved. Finally, he was given alcohol deceitfully and killed by the wretched Ghatams. They also wanted to abort their pregnant sister Yashoda, and sent a midwife to her for that purpose. The midwife took pity on Yashoda. She showed Ghatams a pail of red betel spittle and convinced them that the child has been aborted, thus saving the life of their sister Yashoda.

The sad queen then went to King Brijman to save her life. He asked her to marry him. The queen answered, 'I am your sister's daughter-in-law. You should be ashamed of proposing marriage to me.' In anger, he ordered that she should be hung in the middle of a dense jungle. Hemad Modi, a very rich merchant, thought of a way to save the queen from the king's torture. He said to the king, 'Your Highness, my sister fought with her sister-in-law and has left her home. Why have you ordered her to be hung? What is the reason for her punishment?' The king was puzzled. He placed Hemad Modi in charge of the queen Yashoda and let her go. She lived with him as his sister, and Modi's business began to flourish remarkably.

After sometime, Yashoda gave birth to a son who was God's incarnation. He began to speak right at the moment of his birth. He stopped the midwife from cutting his naval cord. He said, 'Devi will do it,' and the great goddess in fact did. The pundits of Kasipur made his horoscope and named him Chhatri Ghughulia. They said, 'Look Modi, your nephew is of a Kshatriya family. He will earn a lot of recognition. He will make Raja Brijman pay fifty-two lakh of rupees and will marry his daughter.'

When Chhatri Ghughulia was twelve years old, he began to bathe in the Ganges, and placed his *dhoti* on a high rock while he was in the water. At this very time, the Goddess Mother Sharada appeared in the guise of an old woman. She picked up his *dhoti*. The boy asked for the *dhoti*, but she did not give him. He politely said, 'I have only a handful of *puja* rice to offer. I will offer you that if you give my *dhoti* back.' The Devi waited for a little while and then said, 'I cannot eat food cooked by you. You are contaminated because your paternal uncles, the Ghatams, killed your father and did not perform the funeral rites.' The boy became red with anger. By the grace of Devi, he learned the entire story. And by the Devi's grace, he took revenge upon everyone.

He arrived in Ghatampur in the guise of a saint and sat near *Chaura Enara* (well). He said to a girl who had come to fetch water, 'The water of this well stinks, because your wretched king killed his sister's husband by foul play and did not perform the funeral rites.' The girl told the whole story to the Ghatams, and the brothers became worried. They consulted the wandering saint, and asked how they could mitigate their sinful offence. The saint said, 'Feed eighty

Brahmins, and give away as alms the haikal horse and the iron outfit which your brother in law had when you killed them.' The Ghatams did this right away.

As soon as he received their alms, Chhatri Ghughulia put on the iron outfit, he tied fifty-six daggers to his waist, and mounted the flesh-eating haikal horse. He took out his sword and introduced himself to the Ghatams. Then he arrived at Devi's temple and asked her permission to take revenge from Ghatams. She appeared before him and said, 'First ask Brijman to pay fifty-two lakh of rupees to Hemad Modi, who is your uncle and also to marry his daughter.'

He came to Brijman's court. King Brijman heard what he wanted and became very angry. He said to his messenger, 'A mosquito has come to the court. Grind him as you would a paste.' However, Chhatri Ghughulia killed not only the messenger but also Brijman's entire army. In a single moment, the haikal horse consumed fourteen thousand men. There was one survivor: Puranmal Divan, a clerk, who somehow managed to flee with his life. The victorious Ghughulia went to the king. The king was very scared and he paid fifty-two lakh rupees to him. He also married his daughter Sukhanti to Chhatri. After his marriage he, with his wife and Hemad Modi, departed.

The king Brijman played a game. He sent a letter to Delhi that explained Chhatri Ghughulia's *barat* (wedding procession) was traveling, and requested help seizing the fifty-two lakh of rupees from Hemad Modi, chopping off his head, and making the queen Sukhanti a Muslim.

Puranmal Divan and his army caught up to the *barat*. He surrounded the queen's red palanquin. She started crying. Right away, the Mother Goddess Devi woke Ghughulia up and brought him there. By the Devi's blessings, he and his divine brave horse killed all his enemies. Again, only Puranmal Divan fled.

Very soon afterwards, Chhatri Ghughulia was sleeping in his gold bed. Puranmal entered the room and chopped off his head. The lamenting queen Sukhanti took her husband to

Dehuli Jungle and started decorating the pyre. Devi Sharada in the guise of an old woman examined her chastity. She passed. Then Devi went to Queen Yashoda and said, 'Your son has been killed in Dehuli Jungle. Pick him up and bring him to my temple.' Yashoda brought her son's dead body to the temple and began to pray, 'Oh mother Goddess! Please make my son live again. I will worship you with Basmati rice, sandalwood, and I will make a ritual sacrifice of a black goat.' Devi put a sheet of flowers on the brave man. He woke up and sat down and said, 'Mother, order me to chop off the heads of all the uncles and bring them here.' Devi said, 'Do it after some time.'

After some time the barber brought invitation for a *Chhathi* (six days after child birth) in Ghatampur to Chhatri Ghughulia. Yashoda did not want him to go, but in spite of that, he went to Ghatampur like a brave man. The uncles played many tricks on him, but his youngest aunt told him of all his uncles' treacherous plans and secrets. Cleverly he returned home to live happily. One day Queen Sukhanti went to bathe in Sera *Pokhra* (pond). Here all the seven Ghatam brothers were fishing in the pond. They tried to flirt with the queen. Sudhu Mahra ran to the king and told him. He came to the pond's bank. He chopped-off the heads of five uncles. He did not kill his youngest uncle—he only chopped-off his nose, because he was obligated to his youngest aunt. After this, he returned to Hemad Modi's house and began to live happily.

Queen Yashoda tried to please the Devi Goddess by offering her prayers and sacrifices. Devi Sharada blessed Chhatari Ghughulia by putting her hands on his head, and permitting him to live a long and prosperous life.

Kunwar Vijayee

Kunwar Vijayee was very strong and brave from the time of his childhood onwards. He lived with his mother and his sister-in-law. His mother was Gheghamanti, his sister-in-law—his brother's wife—was Sonaamanti, and his father, of whom his female relatives never spoke, was GhoRmal Singh. The name of his mansion was Saurang-garh. He used to play in Ali's *maidan* (field) with children. One day while playing *gulli-danda* (children's game played with a stick and smaller wood) they got into fight. One of them said, 'You have been a villain since your childhood. The fight that took place in your wedding never got settled. Your father, brother and fifty-two lakh of people on the boy's side are jailed in BaavangaRh, and are suffering even today.'

Hearing this Kunwar Vijayee in anger threw his *gulli danda* away—it fell in BaavangaRh's turret, and the turret broke. After this, he ran to his house and began to ask his mother and sister-in-law about the real story. His mother told him, 'Twelve years ago you got married in BaavangaRh. Your father-in-law had asked for fifty-two lakh of men. One person was missing from your *barat*. Because of that, your father-in-law put them in a jail. From then we are all living our lives dependent on you.' Kunwar Vijayee said, 'Mother, do not consider me an ordinary child. I am incarnation of *Bhairav* (God). Give me the sword, I will go and fight alone.' The mother showed his father's swords, which were kept in fifty rooms. But Kunwar did not like any, so the mother took him to an ironsmith to get a very special sword. The ironsmith said, 'How can he fight all by himself?' But when Kunwar insisted, the man built a sword for him, which weighed eighty maunds. The ironsmith blessed him, and then he went with his mother to a temple. The Goddess and his mother blessed him in the temple.

In the palace, he put on an iron suit for fighting. On the head, he wore iron armor, and on his back he had a leather shield. On both of his sides, he had knives and daggers; on the head he had saffron colored turban; and in his hand he had the heavy eighty-maund sword. He bowed before his mother and sister-in-law, saluted them, and left for BaawangaRh.

In the middle of the forest, he ran into Gorakhnath, and touched his feet even though Gorakhnath had his leather shoes on. Gorakhnath blessed him and said, 'Son, you will certainly achieve victory. But the ceremonial bringing of your wife from her father's house will be bad for you, as you will die. But don't worry. Your sister-in-law has nectar flowing through her hands, and will revive you.' Then Kunwar went to the Devi's temple. She blessed him and said, 'Son, my shadow and seven hundred female ascetics will help you. Your first stop will be at the pond *Sairo Pokhra*. He saluted Devi and arrived at BaawangaRh.'

He tied his female Hichli horse on to Ashoka tree. He himself sat under that tree and began to think, 'How do I begin this battle?' At this moment, Devi appeared before him and said, 'By the side of Sairo Pokhra there is a very dense garden. Pluck all the flowers there because the queen worships with those flowers. When you pick flowers, a "Chilhki," a female barber, and a "Salki," a female gardener, will appear. Queen Tilakdei will appear to claim the flowers. But you better be very careful with the woman. The battle will take place under the pretext of these flowers.' Kunwar did exactly what he was told. Chilhki and Salki saw Kunwar. They became suspicious of him. The king of BaawangaRh heard all the news and got very angry.

Kunwar looted the king's Tirpanpatti Bazaar. The king's son Manikchand came with his army and fought. Kunwar cut-off his head and threw it to BaawangaRh. In the palace, grief and distress spread all over. At this very time, he entered the prison and there he released fifty-two lakh of soldiers, the king and his brother, and sent them to Sorang-gaRh. He himself rode the Hichli horse and arrived at the gate fighting. From there, he arrived at the entrance. There, armies surrounded him, but he wielded his sword until in no time he killed the huge army. Then the son-in-law and father-in-law fought. The father-in-law got killed. The entire fort was empty except for the womens' sorrows and crying. Kunwar began to break turrets, and then the queen said, 'Why are you breaking them? Now only the son-in-law and the daughter remain. Now it is your duty to care for the fort.' Kunwar very politely saluted the queen and said, 'You are like my own mother. Now let my wife Tilakdei leave.' The queen, decorating herself, started thanking Devi, and said, 'Because of you, the Goddess, my *gauna* (ceremonial departure) is taking place. I will pray to you with fifty-six kinds of food, and I will give your female ascetics seven hundred black goats to sacrifice.'

As soon as Kunwar came out with Tilakdei, he died. Tilakdei fainted of grief. The pregnant wife of one of the soldiers Kunwar had killed, Manikchand, took revenge on Kunwar. She approached his dead body, chopped-off the head, and threw the body into a well. The magical Hichli horse saw all of this happen. She immediately flew to Sorang-gaRh and related the entire episode to Kunwar's family. There also, people became grief-stricken. Sonaamanti arrived at BaavangaRh with the Hichli horse. She looked for Kunwar's body, but Manikchand's wife slickly said, 'We did his funeral rites.' Queen Tilakdei was in faint and could not answer, but Sonaamanti came to know about the mysterious event from the Hichli horse. She killed Manikchand's wife, removed Kunwar's body from the well, and spilled nectar drops from her hands onto his body. Kunwar was revived. Happiness prevailed all over. Kunwar Vijayee became the king of BaavangaRh and Sorang-gaRh. Kunwar prayed to Devi, 'All of this transpired because of you. All hail to Goddess Durgaa.'

Bibliography

Aryani, Sampatti (1965), *Magahi Vyaakaran Kosh*. Delhi: Hindi Sahitya Sansar.

——— (1976), *Magahi Bhaashaa aur Saahitya*. Patna: Bihar Rashtra Bhaashaa Parishad.

Battle, Kemp P. (1989), *American Folktale*. New York: Simon and Schuster.

Basham A.L. (1954), *The Wonder that was India*. New York: Grove Press Inc.

Breton, Roland J.L. (1997), *Atlas of the Languages and Ethnic Communities of South Asia*. Walnut Creek L.A: Alta Mira Press.

Chaudhury, P.C. Roy (1976), *Folklore of Bihar*. Delhi: National Book Trust.

——— (1982), *Folktales of Bihar*. Delhi: Sahitya Akademi.

Cardona, G. (1974), 'The Indo Aryan Language', *Encylopedia Brittanica*, 15th edn., 9: 439–50.

Chatterji, Suniti Kumar (1926), *The Origin and Development of Bengali Language*, 3 vols. London: George Allen and Unwin (rpt. 1970).

Cole, Joanna (1982), *Best Loved Folktales of the World*. New York: Anchor Books Doubleday.

Crooke, William C. (1894), *Introduction to Popular Religion and Folklore of North India*. Allahabad: Government Press.

Dorson, Richard M. (ed.) (1975), *Folktales Told Around the World*. Chicago: University of Chicago Press.

Dundes, Alan (1980), *Interpreting Folklore*. Bloomington: University Press.

——— (1989), *Folklore Matters*. Knoxville: University of Tennessee Press.

Dundes, Alan (ed.) (1992), *The Evil Eye*. Madison: University of Wisconsin Press.

Das, Jogesh (1972), *Folklore of Assam*. Delhi: National Book Trust.

Flueckiger, Joyce Burkhalter (1996), *Gender and Genre in the Folklore of Middle India*. Ithaca: Cornell University Press.

Grierson, George A. (1884), 'Some Bihari Folksongs', *Journal of The Royal Asiatic Society of England*, vol. XVI.

——— (1903–28), *Linguistic Survey of India*, vols. I-XI. Calcutta; rpt. 1968, Delhi: Motilal Banarsidass.

Goswami, Prafulladatta (1980), *Talks of Assam*. Gauhati: Publication Board, Assam.

Grimes, Barbara F. (1996), *Ethnologue*. Houston: Summer Institute of Linguistics.

Handoo, Jawaharlal (1989), *Folklore: An Introduction*. Mysore: Institute of Indian Languages.

Jackson, A.M.T. and R.E. Enthoven (1989), *Folklore of Gujarat*. Vipin Jain For Vintage Books.

Jeffers, Robert J. (1976), 'The Position of the Bihari Dialects in Indo Aryan', *Indo-Iranian Journal* 18: 215–25.

Katre, S.M. (1968), *Problems of Reconstruction in Indo-Aryan*. Simla: Indian Institute of Advanced Study.

Mathur, G.L. (1992), *Folklore of Rajasthan*. Jodhpur: Books Treasure.

Maity, P.K. (1988), *Folk Ritual of Eastern India*. Delhi: Abhinav Publication.

Nakra, Harishchander (2002), *Wichhada Watan*. Bangalore: W.Q. Press

Nambisan, Vijay (2000), *Bihar*. New Delhi: Penguin Books.

Narayan, Kirin (1997), *Mondays on the Dark Night of the Moon*. Oxford: Oxford University Press.

——— (1989), *Storytellers, Saints, and Scoundrels*. Philadelphia: University of Pennsylvania Press.

Pandeya, Ras Bihari (1982), 'Magahi Bhaashaa ke Adi Kavi Sarahapad', in Ras Bihari Pandeya (ed.), *Magahi Bhaashaa Saahityik Nibandhaawalii*. Patna: Lok Sahitya Sangam.

Pandey, Shyam Manohar (1982), *The Hindi Oral Epic Canainii*. Allahabad: Sahitya Bhawan.

——— (1987), *The Hindi Oral Epic Lorikaayan*. Allahabad: Sahitya Bhawan.

Pandharipande, Rajeshwari (1990), *The Eternal Self and The Cycle of Samśaara*. Needham Heights: Ginn Press.

Panikkar, K.M. (1963), *A Survey of Indian History*. Delhi: Asia Publishing House.

Perricone, Nicholas (2004), *Perricone Promise*. New York: Warner Books.

Prakashi, Mira (1973), *Folktales of Bihar*. Delhi: Sterling Publishers, Pvt. Ltd.

Prasad, Vishvanath (1962), *Magahi Sanskaar Geet*. Patna: Bihar Rashtrabhasha Parishad.

Ramanujan, A.K. (1986), 'Two Realms of Kannada Folklore', in *Another Harmony*, ed. S.H. Blackburn and A.K. Ramanujan. Berkeley: University of California Press, pp. 41–57.

——— (1997), *A Flowering Tree*. Stuart Blackburn and Alan Dundes (eds.). Berkeley: University of California Press.

——— (ed.) (1991), *Folktales from India*. New York: Pantheon Books.

Rao, Velcheru Narayana, Sanjay Subrahmanyam and David Dean Shulman (1998), *Symbols of Substance*. Oxford: Oxford University Press.

Singh, Ram Prasad (1997), *Magadh ki Lok-kathayen*. Gaya: Magahi Academy.

Spear, Percival (1965), *A History of India 2*. New York: Penguin Books Ltd.

Stein, Burton (2001), *A History of India*. New Delhi: Oxford University Press.

Tandan, Prakash (1961), *Punjabi Century, 1857–1947*. Berkeley: University of California Press.

Thapar, Romila (1968), *A History of India*, vol. 1. Maryland: Penguin Books.

Verma, Manindra K. (1971), *The Structure of the Noun Phrase in English and Hindi*. Delhi: Motilal Banarsidass.

——— (1990), 'Experiencer Subjects in Bhojpuri and Magahi', in Manindra K. Verma and K.P. Mohanan (eds.), *Experiencer Subjects in South Asian Languages*. Stanford: CSLI, Stanford University, pp. 85–103.

——— (1991 a), 'Exploring the parameters of agreement', *Language Sciences* 13.2: 125–43.

——— (2003), 'Bhojpuri', a chapter in George Cardona and Dhanesh Jain (eds), *The Indo-Aryan Languages*. London & New York: Routledge, pp. 515–37.

Verma, Sheela and Manindra K. Verma (1983), 'The Auxiliary with Special Reference to Magahi', *Indian Linguistics* 44: 97–101.

Verma, Sheela (1985), *The Structure of the Magahi Verb*. New Delhi: Manohar.

——— (1985), *Magahi Bhasha ki Kriya Sanrachana ka Bhasha Vaigyanik Adhyayan*. Allahabad: Sahitya Bhavan Pvt. Ltd.

——— (2003), 'Magahi', a chapter in George Cardona and Dhanesh Jain (eds), *The Indo-Aryan Languages*. London & New York: Routledge, pp. 498–514.

——— (in Press), An invited chapter (2006) on *Magahi* in the volume *Languages of the World: Modern Indo-Aryan Languages*, ed. Leonid Kulikov, Aleksander Rusakov and Tatiana Oranskaia. Moscow: Russian Academy of Sciences.

Vidyarthi, S.P. and Pandit Ganesh Chaubey (eds.) (1971), *Bihar in Folklore Study*. Calcutta: Indian Publications.

Vidyarthi, L.P. (ed.) (1973), *Essays in Indian Folklore*. Calcutta: Indian Publications.

Winternitz, Maurice (1972), *History of Indian Literature*, vol. I. Delhi: Oriental Publishers and Booksellers.

Wolpert, Stanley (1989), *A New History of India*. Oxford: Oxford University Press.